One of Seventeen

CATHERINE NAGLE

BALBOA PRESS
A DIVISION OF HAY HOUSE

Copyright © 2019 Catherine Nagle.

All rights reserved. No part of this book may be used or reproduced by any means, graphic, electronic, or mechanical, including photocopying, recording, taping or by any information storage retrieval system without the written permission of the author except in the case of brief quotations embodied in critical articles and reviews.

Balboa Press books may be ordered through booksellers or by contacting:

Balboa Press
A Division of Hay House
1663 Liberty Drive
Bloomington, IN 47403
www.balboapress.com
1 (877) 407-4847

Because of the dynamic nature of the Internet, any web addresses or links contained in this book may have changed since publication and may no longer be valid. The views expressed in this work are solely those of the author and do not necessarily reflect the views of the publisher, and the publisher hereby disclaims any responsibility for them.

The author of this book does not dispense medical advice or prescribe the use of any technique as a form of treatment for physical, emotional, or medical problems without the advice of a physician, either directly or indirectly. The intent of the author is only to offer information of a general nature to help you in your quest for emotional and spiritual well-being. In the event you use any of the information in this book for yourself, which is your constitutional right, the author and the publisher assume no responsibility for your actions.

Any people depicted in stock imagery provided by Getty Images are models, and such images are being used for illustrative purposes only.
Certain stock imagery © Getty Images.

Print information available on the last page.

ISBN: 978-1-9822-3295-5 (sc)
ISBN: 978-1-9822-3297-9 (hc)
ISBN: 978-1-9822-3296-2 (e)

Library of Congress Control Number: 2019911744

Balboa Press rev. date: 10/21/2019

Dedication

To my beloved parents, Carmen and Amelia DeNofa and sixteen loving siblings: Carmen, Adeline, Faye, Amelia, Rose, Dominic, June, John, Ernest, Maryann, Robert, Louis, Charles, Thomas, Ronald and Shirley. And to my husband, William, and children, Natalie and William Jr., son-in-law Sean, and grandchildren, Christian and Angelina.

To Ernest, for his extraordinary and loving contributions to our entire family.

And to June, for being the wind beneath my wings!

"And who are all these young men
and women on each side?'
'They are her sons and daughters.'
'She must have had a very large family, Sir.'
'Every young man or boy that met her became
her son—even if it was only the boy that
brought the meat to her back door. Every
girl that met her was her daughter.'
'Isn't that a bit hard on their own parents?'
'No. There are those that steal other people's children.
But her motherhood was of a different kind. Those
on whom it fell went back to their natural parents
loving them more... Every beast and bird that
came near her had its place in her love. In her they
became themselves. And now the abundance of life
she has in Christ from the Father flows over into
them.... Already there is joy enough in the little
finger of a great saint such as yonder lady to waken
all the dead things of the universe into life."
C.S. Lewis
— A scene from The Great Divorce

Contents

Preface	Why So Many Children?	xi
Chapter 1	The Clothes, Hair, and Temperaments They Wore	1
Chapter 2	A Necessary Change of Habits	14
Chapter 3	The Boys Club	26
Chapter 4	Sisters and Sunday Promises	31
Chapter 5	Made for Each Other	44
Chapter 6	Along Comes Sweet Noelle	55
Chapter 7	Letting Go	64
Chapter 8	Crying in the Attic	71
Chapter 9	Uptown	83
Chapter 10	The Truth, Sad Story of Uncle Richard	87
Chapter 11	Settling the Unrest	95
Chapter 12	No More Pretending	105

About the Author 133
About My Writing 135
Synopsis: One of Seventeen 137
Acknowledgments 139

Preface

Why So Many Children?

I was one of seventeen children, all basically orphans who were adopted by our very unusual parents. This really is my story, but to understand me, you first have to know something about them.

Our parents first met in the 1930s and this is the story of our family. Our dad, Carmen Eden, was a handsome, curly-haired paperboy who delivered newspapers on his bicycle. Our mom, Amelia, and our dad were teenagers when they met, and their attraction was lasting. But they lost touch when Carmen grew up and no longer delivered newspapers. They didn't see each other again for several years.

Carmen and Amelia saw each other again when Amelia was visiting her Aunt Katherine, her mother's older sister, one weekend. She'd raised Amelia from infancy after her parents died in a car accident that was caused by a driver who'd been under the influence of alcohol. Aunt Katherine was left to raise the baby, never married, and raised Amelia alone.

When the two saw each other again, Carmen was visiting his friend, who happened to live next door to Aunt Katherine. Carmen and Amelia started talking and soon began dating.

Amelia was a beautiful, dark-haired girl with high cheekbones and a flawless complexion. She didn't wear any make-up, only a little lipstick. She was studying to become a nurse at the Women's Nursing College when they began to see each other exclusively. Carmen now worked as a manager for the important Yale Rail Line.

During the first year that they dated, Carmen and Amelia were too busy to see each other very often, and Carmen's demanding job took him out of town for weeks at a time. This helped Amelia to stay focused on finishing nursing school.

Carmen told Amelia that he had no family. He'd said only that he'd lost all of them and refused to talk about it. He kept his past hidden, and Amelia didn't let his secretiveness interfere with their relationship. She trusted that someday he'd open up about his past but never expected the heartbreaking truth that eventually came out.

Aunt Katherine died during the first year that Carmen and Amelia were together. Amelia and Carmen, both alone, supported each other and soon married. Then Amelia sold her aunt's house and moved into Carmen's large house, which he'd bought using his inheritance.

Unfortunately, Amelia couldn't have children, but she'd always wanted a large family, having grown up as an only child and wanting to enjoy what she'd missed. Carmen also wanted a large family after having no one for so long.

The Edens got their huge family by adopting seventeen children, from newborn to age fourteen. Why did they take in so many children? Because two large, needy families of kids were all put up for adoption at the same time. They had been in and out of foster care for a while and Amelia knew about the tragic circumstances from taking care of them at the health clinic where she worked. During that time, she had grown fond of all of the children. Especially to Caitlin, who seemed very timid.

She'd often brought special gifts for everyone after visits to the clinic. She even sometimes visited at the orphanage and brought new clothes or other treats.

After Carmen and Amelia decided to adopt, they wanted to keep all the children of both families together. So, after a lot of red tape and legal wrangling, they were given permission to adopt every child from both families. They were well-off enough to be able to afford such a large family and any help they'd need to manage with so many children.

Amelia decided to put her nursing career on hold to take care of the large, new family. She had a lot of experience taking care of sick children in the clinic and was confident that the older kids' help would be enough in raising that many children, especially since they were siblings.

The Eden estate was in a secluded area outside of Philadelphia, a few miles away from the center of town. It was formerly called The Manor House by the previous owners.

Carmen bought the large three-story stone house, which was built in the early 1900s, and renovated it long before he ever reconnected with Amelia. It sat on three acres and had a wrap-around porch. It featured seven bedrooms, four baths, and a center-hall staircase. The top floor was a huge room with a high ceiling and exposed rafters that Carmen used for storage. The children shared bedrooms: three were girls' rooms and three were for boys. There were two or three beds in each room, and Carmen and Amelia had their own private bedroom on the second floor.

When he first bought it, the mansion was Carmen's haven, a refuge from the stress of helping to build the Yale Rail Line. At that time, he buried himself in his work, almost hiding from something. But now, with a wife and huge family, the house and setting couldn't be more perfect. Soon it was bustling with activity.

When we were adopted, the clan included Carson, fourteen; Adele, fourteen; Faith, thirteen; Macy, thirteen; Rachel, twelve; Dom, twelve; Josh, ten; Julie, eight; Caitlin, six; Ellis, six; Madison, five; Rob, four; Luke, four; Chas, three; Timothy, two; Ron, one; and Stacey, newborn.

Every day at the Eden house had its share of the usual growing pains, tears and laughter, disappointments, excitement, or adventure. And soon the children no longer felt like orphans. They knew their new parents loved them and their adopted siblings. And despite their differences, they all blended well.

The Edens' clan of adopted children came from two families, each family having been torn apart by alcohol. Caitlin was one of nine children from one family and their mother had died during childbirth. Their father was already absent from their lives, having deteriorated into alcohol addiction. The other eight children had been put up for adoption when their divorced mother's drinking problem kept her from being able to take care of them; she soon disappeared from their lives. And so this lost group of kids now became part of the large and loving Eden family.

Amelia, at home with her younger ones, didn't have the freedom to even shop for groceries. And they could very well afford to have everything delivered, so that's what she did. She never wanted to learn how to drive and was satisfied spending her days cleaning, doing laundry and cooking. She also spent time building her children's self-confidence, encouraging their talents in the same way her Aunt Katherine had done for her.

1
The Clothes, Hair, and Temperaments They Wore

The sweltering August days were coming to an end. In one more week, the County Line Pool would close until next summer season, and it would be time to get ready for school. Caitlin Eden spent every day of her summer vacation in a bathing suit, her eyes bloodshot from the chlorine in the swimming pool. She kept a bathing cap folded inside her towel, ready for water ballet practice or swim-team competition. On her off days, or when the boys swam separately, she was home with some of her brothers and sisters.

Amelia didn't end up hiring outside help with her children and probably didn't delegate as many chores to her older children as she might have. Instead, she hoped to give all of her kids the kind of attention Aunt Katherine had given her.

Teenage Caitlin was active and adventurous, and always looking for ways to make her younger siblings happy. And reading was her refuge. It calmed her down when she became over-excited and couldn't stop talking. But her mom Amelia was especially attuned to Caitlin and knew how to bring out her talents, just as she did with each of her children.

Before school opened, Amelia asked Caitlin to make a list of the younger boys' clothing sizes so she'd know what to buy them for the new school year. Naturally, they grew out of everything, and their clothes from the previous year were too worn out to pass down to the youngest ones.

Then Amelia asked Caitlin to go to the department store and buy all their school clothes.

Caitlin excitedly agreed and Amelia told her what to put on her shopping list.

Amelia pointed out that Ron needed shoes but was too sick to go to the shoe store.

Amelia thought for a moment. Then came up with the solution.

She had Ron stand on a piece of paper and traced his feet. Then Amelia handed Caitlin Ron's perfectly outlined footprints. Caitlin was impressed by her mother's cleverness.

Amelia also gave Caitlin a worn pair of oxfords and asked her to get new ones in brown or dark tan to match the clothes she'd pick out.

Caitlin put the tracings of her brother's feet into a bag and headed uptown to shop.

She felt important because her mother had asked her to go shopping for the boys by herself. She was just thirteen, but had already learned to be a good shopper. She was proud that her mother had noticed her enthusiasm for doing these kinds

One of Seventeen

of errands. And from that day on, Caitlin did the clothes shopping for the younger kids.

❦

One day, Caitlin overheard her mother talking to her older sister, Julie, about her in a way that made her take an honest look at herself. It was something she never forgot.

"Caitlin's very bright, but in many practical ways, not as smart as you, Julie, or some of our other girls. She lacks certain qualities that I'm concerned about, and she seems immature when it comes to boys. I worry about her and how she'll manage when it's time to meet someone to marry. She's almost childlike in that way. On the other hand, she never complains or ask for things, and she's very sweet and fearless."

"I've noticed this silliness of hers. What do you think we should do about it?" Julie asked, pleased at her mom's compliment.

"I don't really know," Amelia said. "Maybe she's too busy with other things so that romance isn't very important to her yet. She's just not typical of girls her age. Most of the girls I knew at the nursing school showed more interest in boys than they should. But I also know firsthand that romantic love does change a person forever!"

"You're right, Mom," Julie said. "I've also noticed when groups of us girls are in our rooms together,

Catherine Nagle

we talk about boys most of the time, but Caitlin isn't very enthusiastic and only listens half-heartily. She also doesn't share her feelings with any of us, either, unless we're talking about the latest fashions or current events. Then she's always interested and you can't shut her up!"

"Yes," Amelia agreed. "She does take a strong interest in the issues on the news. And she loves shopping for things that will make us all happy. I guess that's her way of expressing her love."

◆

There were plenty of secrets that the girls talked about in their rooms, ones that they kept to themselves. One night, they were all giggling when Macy, one of their mischievous older sisters, who they all thought looked like a movie star, taught them how to smoke cigarettes. While she was teaching them to inhale, she couldn't stop laughing at them for coughing, not only because they weren't doing it right, but also because they looked ridiculous. They were all angry at Macy for making fun of them, even though they kept on trying to smoke one cigarette after another, hoping to get it right!

They were smart enough to keep the windows open to let the smoke out so their parents wouldn't catch on. But Amelia found out about the smoking

One of Seventeen

anyway, having found a pack of cigarettes in Macy's pocket when she was doing the laundry.

"Macy! What do you have to say about these cigarettes that I found in your pocket? How on earth did you get them?" Amelia demanded.

Macy told her, "You want to know how I got them, Mother? I just wait for our grocery deliveries. Then I sweet-talk the delivery boy into bringing me cigarettes in exchange for kisses. Everyone smokes these days, even on TV! And smoking makes me look more sophisticated. Besides, it's the latest thing to do!"

All the girls, upon hearing Macy's answer, tried to hide their shock over Macy's bold way of speaking to their mother. They also were impressed by the power that Macy knew she had over men. Her beauty could lure anyone, and she usually got what she wanted, even from the saintliest of men!

Angry, Amelia said, "Well, we'll see that from now on, you'll be too busy to flirt with the delivery boys and smoke cigarettes! And just wait until your father comes home. He'll know exactly what to do about this!"

Still, that didn't stop Macy from approaching the delivery boys again. And just the week *before* Amelia found out about the cigarettes, Macy had already asked one of them to bring her several bottles of hair dye along with the groceries. When it came time for their next delivery, and before their father got home, Macy hid behind the back door and waited. That way she was able to grab her hair dye packaged separately for Macy by the delivery boy. Clutching the bag, she quickly kissed him, then ran to hide the dye in her room.

Caitlin wanted to change her hair color, too, and Macy would help her. So, later that week, when everyone was sitting at the dinner table enjoying their meal, Amelia noticed Caitlin's brightly colored hair. She was astonished.

"Caitlin, I think you've been spending too much time in the sun! Your hair is turning orange," Amelia exclaimed

"I don't think it's from the sun, Mom," she said. "I was spending a lot more time at the pool, practicing for my junior lifeguard's certificate. The chlorine in the water can change hair-color, too!"

"Yes, that could surely do it," Amelia said. "But don't you have to wear a bathing cap? Even with the cap, your hair's pretty bright."

"Yes, I do wear the bathing cap when I'm swimming. But when I was taking Chas or Ellis with me to teach them how to swim, I didn't always wear my bathing cap. I don't wear it when I'm teaching," Caitlin explained, proud of herself.

"Yes, Caitlin. That was very thoughtful of you to bring them along and teach them how to swim. I'm also pleased that you passed your swim test and earned your Junior Lifeguard Certificate," Amelia said with pride.

One of Seventeen

Meanwhile, the other girls at the table struggled to hold back their giggling. Unlike their mom, they all knew why Caitlin's hair was bright orange. But they wouldn't betray Macy or tell their mother that she was the one who had dyed Caitlin's hair!

Caitlin was the first girl Macy experimented on because she decided to trust Macy. She assumed Macy knew best when it came to beauty because she was so beautiful herself. Macy had the sculptured face of a fashion model, with thick, wavy black hair, and she always dressed in striking outfits that set off her striking looks, something the girls all learned from Faith, their elder sister who was studying fashion.

Caitlin wasn't as beautiful as Macy or her other sisters, some of whom were quite glamorous. She also had an inferiority complex because of a bump on her nose. She tried to hide it with her curly hair, which she parted to one side. Caitlin had great hopes for that new hair color, thinking that letting Macy dye her hair might take attention away from her nose. She even believed it might soften and straighten her curls. She was excited about the possibilities, even if they weren't realistic.

That night after dinner, once they were alone, Macy explained the problem of the orange hair-color to Caitlin and the rest of the girls who'd gathered in one of their rooms.

"I used too much peroxide in the mixture that turned poor Caitlin's hair orange; I've learned from my mistake and now I know how to make your hair a beautiful shade of auburn like the movie stars have. And I can do it for all of you! But first I'll correct Caitlin's color and show you how it should have come out!"

"I know that once I fix this, Mom will never find out that I was the one who dyed your hair. And she'll really believe it was from all of us being out in the sun," Macy assured them.

After Caitlin's hair was redone, Julie insisted that her hair be dyed next! Macy used the same solution on Julie's lovely, long silky hair that Caitlin so envied, and it turned out a beautiful shade of auburn. After the rest of the girls saw the results, they all wanted their hair colored. Soon, they were all walking around the house with auburn hair, all looking like movie stars. Meanwhile, their mother was convinced their hair was brightened by the sun!

In addition to getting cigarettes and hair dye from the delivery boys, Rachel, Caitlin's older sister, fell in love with one of them and ran away with him! Amelia overheard Macy talking about it and knew it wasn't just another one of Macy's jokes. Macy had been devastated when she found that Rachel's bed was empty and that all of her clothes were gone!

"Oh, my God!" Amelia cried. "Rachel's only seventeen and she ran off and got married!" How

One of Seventeen

on earth could this have happened without me knowing about it?"

Macy told her, "Rachel had mentioned eloping with the delivery boy to me, Mom! But I didn't take her seriously because she was always talking about love and romance!"

Amelia ran downstairs to Carmen and told him everything. But she felt like she had to do more for her daughter.

"Carmen, please find Rachel and her young man. Bring them home so we'll be able to make them understand about the seriousness of marriage. And we especially need them to see that they shouldn't have children at such a young age! And to think, Carmen, we don't even know which delivery boy she married! But we surely must have met him!"

"I'll do the best that I can," Carmen said. "But Amelia, please try not to worry so much until we find out what really happened."

Carmen was clever and knew how to get to the bottom of the situation. He simply waited for the delivery truck to arrive the next day. He planned to ask the driver about the man Rachel had eloped with. He found out the boy's name was Travis, and he was a very respectable and successful young man. Not only that, but he actually owned the delivery service! He'd started it to make something of himself. And actually gave his aging father -level manager's job so he'd feel needed. All of this positive news made everyone feel good about Rachel's new husband.

Next, Carmen called the Travis Delivery Service and talked to Travis. He pleaded for them to come home so everyone could meet Travis and have a chance to talk.

Rachel and Travis came home the next day and Amelia made a special dinner of homemade spaghetti and meatballs to celebrate their homecoming. She wanted to start off this new marriage in the right direction. So the entire family dressed in their Sunday best and sat around their huge dining room table with wide eyes as they listened to Travis, smiling at their new brother-in-law without interrupting or saying a word, and they were all on their best behavior.

After dinner and talking with Travis, everyone understood why Rachel had fallen in love with him. They were all happy, relieved, and glad to welcome Travis into the family. And before long, his warmth and kindness began to enrich all of their lives.

Meanwhile, Caitlin began to feel lost because her sisters were maturing ahead of her in more ways than she'd realized. She recalled how Rachel had always focused on boys, but Caitlin hadn't realized that her sister had meant all the things she'd told her, that a man's love was the answer to all her dreams. She'd proven it by eloping! But Caitlin had never thought that way. She was so different

One of Seventeen

from the rest of her sisters, who all wanted to meet a man and fall in love.

Caitlin wished she could have explained better to Rachel that a man's love wasn't the only kind that they needed. But she hadn't known how. It wasn't until she fell in love herself that she finally understood what her sisters felt.

⬥

One day, Carmen returned home from work in a somber mood. His tone of voice caught Amelia off guard when she tried to talk with him about Macy getting in trouble at school. But Carmen was not in the mood to hear about it and asked if it could wait. Amelia agreed that it wasn't all that serious.

Today, something had happened at the Yale Rail Line that affected Carmen's position. It was the reason Cason was in such a serious mood.

The company was proposing to move Carmen's headquarters, the prime location that he ran. Although this was beneficial for the company, it meant that he would have to relocate, something that would affect the entire family. He didn't want to move the children from the comfort of their new home and their schools, where they were adjusting well. Carmen and Amelia had been fortunate that, with their wealth, they were able to send them in the finest schools.

Catherine Nagle

Amelia sensed something was wrong. "What is it, Carmen?" Amelia asked. "You're too quiet. This isn't like you, so please talk to me!"

"It's my job with the railway, Amelia. The job that I've excelled at for twenty years. Our headquarters is moving," said Carmen! "They're being generous and fair, and they want to transfer me to another territory because I'm only five years away from full retirement. Then I can draw my twenty-five-year pension. They don't want me to lose it. But I've explained to them that I didn't want to move the family," He told her.

Carmen continued: "But then, suddenly, I didn't have to decide on anything! That's because the draft notice I got made my decision for me. I've been notified that I'm to report for duty in the Army!"

Carmen accepted his responsibility to serve in the military with dignity, loyalty, and honor. Many men ages 18-49 were called to serve, even those with big families.

Because of Carmen's much bigger news, Amelia never bothered to tell Carmen about Macy smoking cigarettes in school. It just wasn't that important anymore. Amelia was sure this was just a passing phase, and that Macy would grow out of it. Macy had an innocent temperament and often clowned around, playing tricks on everyone, even her classmates at school. Now Amelia would have to handle this alone and so much more.

One of Seventeen

Not wanting to upset Carmen more than he already was, Amelia had to sweep things under the rug that weren't very serious. She didn't want to bother him with anything trivial before he left for active duty.

2
A Necessary Change of Habits

Amelia began to worry about how to support the family with Carmen going into the Army. Besides Amelia's experience in nursing school, she had worked in a family clinic before she was married, and before they'd adopted all their children. But she didn't know exactly how she could find work to support her huge family now that Carmen was being drafted. For the first time, they were faced with a financial predicament. It was all she thought about.

Some of the children were under sixteen and needed a lot of Amelia's attention. And she was especially concerned about her five very young children. They still depended on her for everything for her to consider leaving them to get a job. After giving it a lot of thought, she came up with a solution that would benefit the family. But it meant changing the habits of everyone in the house.

So, beginning with herself, Amelia was more careful with money. She stretched a penny and everything in the Eden house so that it all worked for everyone. And she came up with ways to get her children involved in helping her and each other.

One of Seventeen

Amelia believed that with so many children, she couldn't offer any valuable outside service to an employer and delegate her household responsibilities. She believed, like most women at the time, that it was her job to take care of her kids, something she loved and accepted from the beginning.

Amelia believed that mothering was her role. From the beginning, she had been the one who wanted to adopt so many children, and she'd gotten her way. Because Carmen had loved her so much and wanted to please her, he'd agreed to it and she never forgot it.

With such a large family, several older kids were about to graduate high school and leave home.

Carson, the oldest boy, was at the top of his class and was an accomplished athlete. He won a baseball scholarship to Florida State and was leaving in September. Faith was in the same high school class and was soon leaving for California, where she'd be going to modeling school, something that had always interested her. Adele, the oldest girl, was engaged to her high school sweetheart and they planned to be married after graduation. They were moving to Ireland, where her husband would take over the family business from his aging grandparents. And Dom already had started his own company, an awning business, and had just gotten engaged to be married. This meant that four of the oldest kids, all high school

Catherine Nagle

graduates, would be leaving at the same time to start their new adult lives. And Rachel was already married and out of the house.

But this still left twelve children, and Amelia would have to raise them alone once Carmen left for the Army. So Amelia came up with a solution that would also build their self-confidence. One by one, she approached each child with ideas and suggestions, beginning with Ellis, who was fifteen.

"Ellis," Amelia began, "Would you like to get an after-school job?"

"I'd love to, Mom, but what kind of job could I possibly get? I'm only fifteen."

"Well, since your dad will be leaving for duty soon, we're going to have to cut back on a lot of things around here. I saw a help-wanted ad in the newspaper for a part-time delivery boy for the market uptown on the avenue to deliver groceries in our neighborhood. I was thinking about how fond you were of your wagon that's still in the garage, and that you might like to use it again to be a delivery boy. And with everyone being drafted these days, other boys will want this job. So you'll need to apply right away."

"That's a good idea, Mom! That job would be great," Ellis said. "And every time I go to work, you can give me a list of things you need. I'll bring them home when I'm done for the day! And it wouldn't interfere with school. I can get my homework done in study hall. Thanks, Mom! I hope I get it!"

One of Seventeen

After dinner that night, Ellis was so excited and hopeful about the job that he brought an old desk down from the attic and fixed it up. He polished it and placed it against the wall in a nook of the kitchen. From that point, Ellis began to grow up and take responsibility. His mother noticed his enthusiasm and gave him a notepad and pencils for his desk. After he applied for the job, he quickly heard back from the market that the job was his and he needed working papers before he could start, since he was under sixteen. After getting the job, he dedicated himself to his delivery route to help his family.

Because Caitlin loved to write, Amelia asked her to write a letter to the school for Ellis's working paper application. As Caitlin was proudly writing the letter for Ellis, she thought about how she, too, could contribute to the family. She didn't know yet what she wanted to do in her career, and unlike her sisters, she had no interest in marrying and having children. But she had always admired and respected her teachers and was drawn to the educated.

Julie overheard her mother talking to Ellis and Caitlin about his after-school job and began to lecture Caitlin about how she could help the family, too. Julie was wise and practical, but sometimes she was really bossy with Caitlin, who was her real sister, and not just through adoption.

Julie suggested that Caitlin get an after-school job at the same place where Julie worked, the Aspen Restaurant uptown.

Although she wanted to help out, Caitlin felt like she'd just been given a jail sentence. She didn't like Julie's suggestion one bit, and also didn't appreciate Julie telling her what to do! She resented Julie pushing her around, something that happened quite frequently. And this was the first time Caitlin realized where her passions really were—in becoming a teacher.

Caitlin tried her best to compose herself and respond kindly, hoping Julie would understand her. She explained that she wanted to study and get her degree and that she hoped to become a teacher one day.

Julie responded by saying teachers were underpaid and that as a waitress, she worked two hours after school and one day on the weekend and earned more money than some teachers make in a week. Julie finished by telling Caitlin about all the money and tips she made, and continued to lecture her sister on her work experience until Caitlin finally backed down.

Julie told Caitlin she was being silly and selfish, and that their parents needed their help now. She said it was no time to prove something, instead of helping the family.

Caitlin walked away and thought about what Julie had said. And the more she thought about it, the more she believed her sister was right. This wasn't the time to think about herself and what she wanted for a career. No. Instead, she'd help bring in some money for the family after everything their parents had done for them!

So, after their father left to join the Army, Julie and Caitlin quit high school. They both became full-time waitresses at the Aspen Restaurant, and for the next few years they helped to keep the Eden family going – along with helping at home. Julie helped with cooking and Caitlin did the shopping and buying clothes.

But no matter what else she was doing, Caitlin kept up her love of learning by continuing to read as much as she could. She even bought herself a typewriter with her tip money and taught herself how to type. Her first real typing job was the daily menus at the restaurant where she worked. She sat proudly typing them in the back booth. She provided her typing service for free in appreciation for letting her practice typing at work when they weren't busy. Her main focus was the money that her family needed and nothing more.

With both girls working full-time, their mother Amelia could stay home with the younger kids. This gave Caitlin a great sense of accomplishment. After all, having that many children was a lot for anyone to handle. Caitlin had helped the kindergarten teacher at her school, where she worked with as many as fifteen children in the classroom, And because her grades were good, she could skip a class and help that teacher. Yet their mother had just as many children at home and took take care of them without any help. This made Caitlin glad that she'd listened to Julie's advice because their mother really needed their help.

Amelia supported and helped all her children, especially now that Carmen was away in the Army. She washed Julie's and Caitlin's uniforms and polished their work shoes so they were always ready for work. And she did everyone else's laundry. When Caitlin and Julie worked late shifts, she asked what they'd like for dinner and had it ready when they walked in the door. The rest of the time she took care of the little ones, keeping them away from Ellis's important papers on his desk so his scheduled delivery route stayed in perfect order. She didn't ask anything more from her children aside from the help they were already giving her. She expected them to be kind and considerate to each other and to do their best at school or at work. And she would be there whenever they needed her.

At last, Carmen came home from the war after being wounded. He was awarded the Purple Heart but unfortunately, he had shrapnel deeply embedded in his back, and he also suffered from emotional problems that were called "shell shock" or battle fatigue at that time.

One of Seventeen

Even with all that had happened to him, Carmen once again took his place and blended back into his family. He helped with all the chores at home, even showing Ellis how to expand his trucking business. In time, that after-school job grew into the successful Eden Construction Company, which in turn helped the family, too. By this time, Ellis was a grown man and a successful go-getter, ready to go out on his own and marry.

And the others grew up, too. Three of the other Eden boys, Josh, Chas, and Luke, all close in age, earned engineering and building scholarships from schools in California. They'd all leave for school in the fall.

Because Julie and Caitlin didn't have their own cars yet, Carmen drove them to and from work every day. He noticed that Caitlin hadn't matured socially and didn't date like the rest of his girls, and it concerned him.

Now that the older ones were either married or starting their own careers, Carmen took over some household jobs. He even started to bake, delighting everyone in the house with his experiments. When he baked his first large tray of cinnamon buns, they were so heavy that they must have weighed five pounds each. Amelia laughed and told her children that he baked more than enough to feed an army!

One day, Stacey, the youngest child interrupted everyone with some exciting news. Rachel and

Travis had pulled into the driveway and there was a baby in the car seat!

Amelia quickly ran and looked out the front window. By this time, she saw Rachel and Travis walking up the long pathway, and Rachel was carrying her baby. Because Rachel and Travis lived far away, it was the first time that anyone saw the new baby. It had been a few years since Rachel had married and moved away. And as Carmen and Amelia had advised, they'd waited a while to start a family. And now, here was little Travis, ready for everyone to meet!

After everyone joyfully greeted Rachel and Travis, and after they all had a chance to play with the baby, everyone sat down for dinner. After their huge cinnamon bun deserts, Travis and Carmen settled down in the living room, and the girls stayed in the kitchen together to finish up clearing the table.

It was then that Rachel asked Madison to help with little Travis. They'd had a long trip and she was very tired. She admitted that taking care of a baby around the clock took a lot out of her.

Madison said she would be happy to help Rachel. She'd been taking child-care classes at school and longed to be married with her own children very soon. Taking care of Travis would be a great experience.

Rachel advised her not to rush to get married. She'd have plenty of time to start her own family when the right time came. She told her to concentrate on her studies first,

Madison reminded her that she was almost the same age Rachel was when she got married. And Rachel told her sister that they'd waited to have children because their Mom and Dad advised it. Rachel warned Madison that having children would definitely change her life forever!

Madison told her that she wasn't interested in doing anything else with her life besides having a husband take care of her and to have children.

Then Rachel told her she had a splendid idea. She asked Madison to consider moving in with her and Travis, and become their part-time nanny for Travis. They were moving back to be closer to the family, and she would be helping Travis by working in the home office they'd set up. She explained that it was the reason they'd made the trip. She was going back to school to get her business degree because she'd realized that there was more to life than romance!

She warned Madison that was why she needed to finish her education. She didn't want her sister to be disappointed by expecting a husband's love to keep making her happy. By living with Travis and Rachel, Madison wouldn't need to take babysitting classes in school anymore. She'd learn how to take care of children by helping with Travis, and earn some extra money. That way she'd help both families. She'd still be able to stay in school, get her high school diploma, and still be close to home. Madison happily accepted Rachel's offer.

As she was clearing the table, Caitlin listened to Madison's talk of wanting to get married and have children at such an early age. Just hearing about it made her uneasy, although she was glad Rachel's advice and firsthand experience had convinced Madison to stay in school and study.

Caitlin loved children too, but she still couldn't believe that romance was the only reason to exist. Maybe it was because her birth father had given her and her eight siblings up for adoption that she saw things differently. She wasn't sure, but she knew she didn't expect anything from anyone other than herself. As dreams of getting married and taking care of children, she was content with helping taking care of her siblings clothing need. Being involved with the younger children's activities wasn't that different from having her own children.

Once Carmen finished talking with Travis, Amelia convinced him that it was a good idea for Madison to be a part-time nanny for their baby grandson. Amelia didn't like the idea of a stranger babysitting for him and was happy that Madison would be taking care of little Travis. She'd been trained in her child-care classes and she was the baby's aunt.

Carmen agreed, but *only* if Madison continued her studies. And then Madison moved into Rachel

One of Seventeen

and Travis's new house, which was near the Eden home. Madison loved living with Rachel and Travis, and she especially enjoyed taking care of baby Travis, and because she got to meet all the delivery boys who worked for the Travis Trucking Company.

Madison still couldn't keep her eyes off the boys! She'd go out of her way to fix up and curl her hair, and always wore lipstick if she was going to see them. She wanted to look her prettiest, knowing these young men would be coming to the Travis home office to pick up their next day's schedules. She soon started dating one of them. A beautiful young lady now, she was also smarter now. Eventually she had a long engagement to one of the company's salesmen, but first, she had to finish her education!

3

The Boys Club

Carmen always looked forward to Sundays, with all the sports on television, and so did his sons. It was their typical Sunday ritual. Amelia would spend the whole morning preparing her usual spaghetti and meatball Sunday dinner, knowing it would bring her family together. Julie took charge of mixing the meatballs. All the girls helped set up the table so mom and Julie could prepare dinner without being too distracted.

By now, even the youngest children were growing up. Ron, the youngest boy, had just completed the tenth grade and had already made up his mind to join the military after graduation. Meanwhile, Rob, just a year older than Ron was proud to have been invited to play in Minor League Baseball (MiLB) in St. Petersburg, Florida, following Carson, his oldest brother. And the youngest girl, Stacey, was already in the ninth grade.

There were only six children living at home at this point, with Madison having moved in with Rachel and Travis. But on Sundays, everyone came over for dinner.

Carmen and the boys looked forward to seeing baby Travis just as much as Amelia and the girls

One of Seventeen

did. That was the one thing all the Edens had in common: their love of children! You'd think that after growing up with so many siblings, having more children around would be the last things they'd want. But it was exactly the opposite.

One time, Adele and her husband Chuck made a surprise visit from Ireland, bringing their two young children, Leia and Chap, for the family to meet for the first time. And for the entire week of their stay at the Eden estate, the whole family gathered around these two little Irish children, treating them like little movie stars!

Early in the formation of the huge Eden family, when the men and boys watched ball games, no women or girls were invited to watch with them. In those days, the guys believed that sports were *not* for women. And if a female came into the room, she would usually excuse herself and quietly go about setting the dinner table or some other necessary activity and then leave. Carmen started out being very strict about keeping the girls away during games on TV because the boys were often loud and tended to speak rudely if their team made an error or lost a game.

But things gradually changed in the Eden house, and in time the men and boys began doing things like cooking and baking now that Carmen was retired and at home much of the time. He set a good example for the boys in the kitchen, beginning with his experiments in baking.

Catherine Nagle

One day, while Amelia and the girls were outside sitting on the porch, enjoying the fresh air, Ron, who was then sixteen, decided he felt like having some bacon. Alone in the kitchen, he put the bacon in the frying pan. While he was waiting for the bacon to crisp, he noticed the fat from the bacon splattering everywhere, including on his face! To protect himself, he put a large brown paper bag over his head with holes cut out for his eyes, nose, and mouth. Then he contentedly finished cooking his bacon.

At that point, Amelia and the girls happened to come back inside and into the kitchen, where they found this ridiculous robot-like character standing in front of the stove.

"Ron, what on earth are you doing with a brown paper bag over your head?" Amelia asked with a laugh.

"I just finished cooking bacon by myself! And, as you can see, I've even figured out how to keep the bacon splatter from burning my face. You ought to try it, Mom!"

Amelia and her girls laughed. For the rest of their lives, they'd always remember Ron standing in front of the stove with that goofy brown paper bag over his head.

The following weekend, Luke, now seventeen and wanting to copy Ron, said he wanted to learn how cook, too, since he was leaving for California in the fall. So, before he even opened the cabinet and reached for a frying pan, he was already cutting holes in a brown paper bag for his eyes, nose, and mouth!

The boys stuck together with their inventions, and they learned lessons from their father and from each other. They even traded ideas. For example, days later, Carmen was drawn into the kitchen by the smell of bacon, which Luke was cooking.

"Luke," Carmen said, "That bacon smells really good! Do you have enough for me, too?"

Feeling proud of himself, Luke told him, "Sure, Dad," and they both sat down and ate together.

Then Carmen said, "Luke, are you going to help clean up this mess you made and learn how to tidy up, now that you're leaving for California?"

And with a hardy laugh, Luke said, "Oh, no, Dad! You know that's not a boy's job. Cleaning is for girls!"

Carmen calmly explained to his son that no, cleaning up wasn't just for girls and that he'd doing it now will better prepare him for college.

Amelia was grateful that her boys were starting to help around the house, she didn't mind helping them learn to clean up the messes they made now that they were cooking some of the time. Amelia stifled a laugh over Luke's obliviousness. She knew how loving, thoughtful, and kind Luke always was to all his sisters.

Catherine Nagle

Amelia had always made excuses for her children, and now she was making even more allowances for them, knowing that some of her boys would be leaving soon for training, college, or the military and she'd miss them. But they all had their own chores, like cutting the three acres of lawns and helping their father with everything mechanical around the house. These were task the girls didn't usually try to tackle. And despite the progress on equality between the boys and girls, they still were stuck with their own, typically female kinds of chores like helping with the house cleaning and doing the dishes. The Eden children had started out being taught to follow traditional, old-fashioned feminine and masculine roles because their parents believed in them. But eventually they learned how to balance and support each other.

The boys were always attentive to their sisters. And they loved to playfully tease the girls, especially by saying that they were the winning team because there were nine boys to eight girls. It was the one way that the boys could never be beaten by the girls!

4

Sisters and Sunday Promises

Macy, one of the older sisters, was still content living at home and helping the family by working at the Florence Candy Factory in center city. She was a born leader and so good at organizing that she was soon promoted to supervisor. She found that she loved managing people. And because she worked in a candy factory, her younger siblings waited for her to come home from work because she'd always bring them candy. Sometimes she paid for it with her company discount, or else she'd bring them the broken candy pieces that employees were allowed to take home. One day, Macy brought home a bag of special giant lollipops. They were six inches in diameter, with licorice and candy drop faces made for the holidays. To the children's delight, all the lollipops had crossed eyes!

Carmen asked her why all the lollypops were cross-eyed. Macy explained that she'd crossed them intentionally. Carmen asked her why and Macy explained.

"I did it because I work alongside Charlotte, one of the kindest women that I've ever met. She's childlike in some ways, but she's bright, and she's worked at the candy factory for years, ever since they opened. She's never been married or had children and she must be in her forties."

"So, when the lollypops came down the conveyer belt, I decorated the first lollypop as an example to the others, and somehow I got the eyes crossed. And just like a little kid, Charlotte couldn't stop laughing. And that's why I made all of the lollypops cross-eyed--just to make her laugh!"

Carmen laughed, enjoying Macy's mischievousness and good-hearted humor, even at work. And he was just as thrilled as the kids to have candy for everyone to enjoy. He had a sweet tooth, too, and he knew Macy just wanted to make the kids happy. She always brought joy to everyone, especially to her younger siblings.

At work, Macy eventually met Saul, the son of the owner of the Florence Candy Factory. He fell in love with her immediately and they married soon after. His family was thrilled that he'd chosen Macy for his wife, not only because she was a tremendous asset to their fine candy business, but also because she made their son so happy. So they loved her, too. But even after she was married, Macy still visited her parents every day and brought them candy and gifts, and always knew how to make them laugh.

Meanwhile, things continued to change at the Eden house as each of the children left the nest. And things changed quite suddenly and unexpectedly for Caitlin when Julie asked her to switch shifts at the Aspen Restaurant. Caitlin was not happy about it and she couldn't hide her feelings.

"That's not fair, Julie!" cried Caitlin when her sister asked her to take her Sunday afternoon shift. "I look forward to my Sundays off, too."

"Well, I'm older than you, so you should let me do what I think best. Remember, I got you this job," Julie hissed.

Caitlin said, "Why should I have to do what you think is best? You're not my boss! And besides, isn't it up to the owner of the restaurant to decide who takes a shift?"

"Yes, it is, and he appointed me head waitress, so it's up to me to make sure all the shifts are covered. Besides, I'm your older sister! I've been helping Mom and Dad with the finances and I've been taking over more responsibility. They are not as young as they used to be. Don't you have any common sense, Caitlin?" Julie asked.

She went on: "Now that I'm twenty-two, I'll be moving in with my boyfriend Anthony because he's asked me to marry him. And then you can take over everything yourself, both in the restaurant and in the house!"

"By myself?" Caitlin cried. "But I really want to do something more with my life than be a waitress. I want to make something of myself and finish school. But I'm not ready for marriage yet, either! Helping with the responsibilities at home should be something we both handle together!" Caitlin said.

Caitlin felt defeated. She knew she couldn't do anything to change the situation. After all, Julie had gotten her the job at the most prestigious restaurant in town, and she did make very good money there, which contributed to running the Eden home. She knew her parents had given up so much to adopt and raise all of them and deserved their help now. And she knew that Anthony had just graduated from medical school and had asked Julie to help him set up his practice. Caitlin convinced herself that it was the right thing to do, so she gave in to Julie's demands and began working on Sundays.

Then, during one of those Sundays when Caitlin would have preferred to do anything other than work, Josh came home for the weekend with his friend James Marino. James was the CEO of Wings Aviation, which was just outside of town. And just like that, working on Sundays became a blessing for Caitlin when she was introduced to her brother's friend.

Josh explained that he'd be home visiting for a few days and was out on the town with his friend James. Then the two friends sat down at the restaurant counter.

Josh asked Caitlin if she'd met James at their house, but she didn't think so. She was sure she'd have remembered him. Caitlin smiled at James

One of Seventeen

and said it was nice to meet him and asked what she could get for him.

James asked for a Coke because it was hot out. And Josh asked for the same thing.

Then he asked his sister what time she was getting off work. Caitlin said, "We close at nine o'clock, thank heavens. I really don't like working on Sundays, and at these late hours, having to call Dad to pick me up."

James told her, "We're going to the movie theater up on the avenue. The show's over at around nine. I have my car and we can take you home if you'd like!"

Caitlin told him she'd really appreciate the ride and James promised to be back at nine.

"I'll call Dad and let him know that you and Josh are driving me home. He'll know I'm safe with the two of you," Caitlin said as they walked out the door.

And so, for the first time, Caitlin didn't mind working the rest her shift as she waited for her brother and James to take her home. And now there was a gleam in her eyes that sparkled as James drove them home. She could hardly take her eyes off him! But she got an even bigger surprise the following Sunday night, when, in walked James just before closing, and this time he was alone!

Caitlin smiled and said hello. She tried to hold back her excitement as he sat at the counter in the same seat as the week before.

James said hello and smiled back.

She asked if he wanted a nice cold Coke and if he'd been to the movie theater.

But James said no to both questions. "I've come by to see if you need a ride home because I can take you. And that way you won't have to bother calling your father. And no, I wasn't at the movies tonight. I'm here because I wanted to see you!"

Caitlin told him, "I'd love to get a ride with you, James! But first I have to clean up and close the restaurant. I also have to call my father to let him know he doesn't have to pick me up, and I hope you don't mind waiting a little longer."

James sat at the counter and watched every move Caitlin made, but he tried to hide it. After she finished cleaning up, she tried to compose herself. She found James quite charming, but she was very nervous and excited having him around. She could barely keep a grip on the key as she locked the front door of the restaurant. She was even stumbled getting into James' car.

Once they were in the car, James asked if he could hold her hands for a moment because he was so nervous in her company! Since it was already late and the drive home a short one, they didn't have much time to get to know each other. And it was almost time for Caitlin's curfew-- another

One of Seventeen

reason Caitlin disliked working on Sundays. By the time she was done with work, it was always too late to do anything but go home and straight to bed. In the Eden household, everyone had to be home and in bed by curfew, regardless of their age!

But, on one of those Sunday nights, after taking Caitlin home for several weeks in a row, James drove in the opposite direction and then parked along a tree-lined road in front of Pennypack Park. He put his arms around Caitlin and told her that he was falling in love with her. They looked into each other's eyes and kissed passionately.

From that day on, James quickly made it his business to be available for Caitlin and took her everywhere with him. They went shopping uptown on the avenue, grabbed a bite to eat, or did whatever else they wanted to do. They soon got to know each other well. But then, James was notified that the government was moving the entire air base to Maryland, and because of that, he would have to relocate Wings Aviation there, too!

James didn't want to leave Caitlin, but he knew he needed to move his company to continue working with the government and be able to grow his business.

So that was when James asked Caitlin to marry him, hoping she'd say yes and go with him to Maryland. She wanted very much to marry him, but she felt that things were moving much too fast.

She knew that her family depended on her income, especially now that Julie would be moving out to get married. So Caitlin told James that she couldn't give him her answer yet because it wouldn't be easy for the family, which depended on her. Although she fully intended to marry James because she truly loved him, she felt that she was abandoning her family!

"Caitlin," James said, "I have a wonderful idea! Let's take a trip to Maryland for a weekend so we can have a look at the new Wings location. It's only a few hours' drives, and we can make it into a long weekend adventure."

"Yes! I'd love to," Caitlin told him. "I'll ask Julie to change shifts with me that weekend. I can't tell her anything else about us. Otherwise, she might tell our parents about our plans, and it's just not the right time to tell anyone yet. I'll tell Julie and my mother that I'm going on a shopping trip to Maryland with a friend to look for a bargain for my dress for Julie's wedding. They'll believe this because they know I'm a very good shopper!"

"You understand my reasons, don't you, James?" Caitlin asked.

"Sure, I do. And when we get to Maryland, I'm planning to have extra time to look at houses for us close to the new airbase," James said.

"That would be great," Caitlin said and sighed with relief.

One of Seventeen

Julie sweetly agreed to switch weekends with Caitlin, especially knowing her sister would be shopping for a dress to wear to the wedding. And Amelia thought it was a wonderful idea to search for bargains in Maryland. She knew Caitlin wasn't frivolous and had an eye for expensive, high-quality items that she always managed to get on sale or at a good discount. She was known to use her money wisely.

James and Caitlin had a wonderful time in Maryland, visiting the new air base and the new location of his aviation business. They looked at houses, too, and James helped pick out the dress she'd wear to Julie's wedding. After she tried it on and showed it to James, she kept it on, believing that the dress echoed their own desire to be married soon, too.

James had booked a lovely room at the Hilton Inn. Caitlin was so anxious and excited that she was in tears when they entered the hotel. James could see by her expression that she'd never been in a hotel room with a man. He reassured her by explaining that he'd never been intimate with a woman before this, and that she would be his first, too. All of Caitlin's inhibitions just melted away. They had eloped and exchanged vows to love each other always. Then they fell into each other's arms and spent a wonderful first night together.

Two days later, on the ride back home, they talked over everything and couldn't wait to share their plans with their families. Caitlin had learned that James came from a successful family of doctors. He'd been raised by a nanny because his parents' jobs were so demanding and critical to their community. James said he, too, had often felt like an orphan for most of his life, despite being part of a prominent family.

But their plans to celebrate with their families came to an abrupt halt when James received a late phone call that he had to fly back to Maryland immediately. The government was providing a special air force plane for him and he had to depart the moment they returned!

The next day, Caitlin received a phone call from James.

He said he was sorry about having to run off so quickly, but that he'd had to sign a new government contract and that they'd also needed the airplane. He said, "The good news is that the contract I signed is for twenty-five years! So we shouldn't have to worry about my future employment for a very long time. We're all set and on our way to starting a new life. I have an even bigger surprise waiting for you here. All it needs is your signature."

Caitlin was thrilled. "James, I'm so happy for the first time! I feel like I'm dreaming! Please promise not to say anything to anyone in my family. I'm going to wait until you get back so we can tell my parents together and do it properly!"

One of Seventeen

"I promise," James said. "Isn't this just wonderful, Caitlin? Everything will have fallen into place by then." They said their loving goodbyes and hung up.

◆

It was late one summer afternoon when James took off from Maryland in the government plane to come back for Caitlin. Storms were popping up everywhere, but James was a trained professional pilot and an expert navigator. He was used to flying with instruments in bad weather, and all during his flight home, he played over in his mind Caitlin's soothing words of endearment.

The next morning, no one expected to hear the shocking and tragic news when someone came pounding on the Edens' front door.

"Carmen, wake up! Someone's at the door," Amelia cried.

"Who on earth could it be at four o'clock in the morning?" Carmen asked. And they both ran downstairs to find out.

A police officer asked to see Caitlin Marino.

"Yes, there's a Caitlin here, but her name is Caitlin Eden," Amelia said, moving closer to Carmen.

She went upstairs to get Caitlin, who quickly grabbed a robe and went down to see what the matter was.

Catherine Nagle

"Please sit down, Mrs. Marino. Your husband James was in a flying accident in the severe thunderstorms last night and his plane crashed. I'm so sorry to tell you that he didn't make it."

"Oh, no! It can't be! Oh my God!" cried Caitlin.

The officers then explained somberly, "We found this house key tag on his key ring. It has your name on it: Mrs. Caitlin Marino. However, the home address is a Maryland address, 1839 Pear Lane, Annapolis, Maryland. We located you from the Maryland marriage license that was with his personal effects, along with your maiden name and address found in the plane's wreckage."

The officers handed Caitlin the house key and the marriage license, and Caitlin ran upstairs to be alone. She lay on her bed, hysterical, the house key clutched tightly in her hand. She begged her parents for some time to be alone. She'd had a glimpse into the mystery of love's resilience and fell exhaustedly into a deep sleep.

After some time, Caitlin came back downstairs and explained everything to her parents about her relationship and marriage to James. She told them she was very sorry she hadn't told them, and that James was actually the friend she'd been seeing and traveling with those past few weeks. She'd been afraid to tell them that she was married because she knew they depended on her help financially. She said all of this through her tears and apologized to them and the rest of her family for not being truthful.

Julie was upset because Caitlin hadn't shared all the intimate details with her first, the way she'd always shared everything with Caitlin. Later, Caitlin privately told Julie that she'd been too embarrassed to talk about romance with anyone, especially with their parents, since the marriage had already happened. After all, she'd always been the immature, inexperienced one in the family when it came to romance, never having understood before the enchantment that it could hold.

5

Made for Each Other

After the heartbreaking funeral and meeting James's family and friends for the first time at the service, Caitlin was lost and in a daze. The following week she went back to work and dragged herself through the days without eating or sleeping much. She was miserable and disliked every second of work, but the money was necessary to the family's survival. Besides, working kept her mind occupied. She kept thinking about how unfair life was and promised herself that she wasn't going to stay drowning in this sorrow for long.

Everyone believed she was living in denial because she had so quickly returned to work. But she felt she knew exactly what she was doing by accepting her responsibility not to burden anyone. And she dressed for the part.

Soon, the briskness of Fall was in the air. All of Caitlin's dreams now hinged on going to college and becoming a teacher. But then, only a month later, she found out she was pregnant with James's baby. And once again she had to change gears. She was overjoyed about her baby and the prospect of becoming a mother. Caitlin believed that this was another sign that her sorrow now needed to be over

As shocking as this news was to Caitlin, it was also a huge concern for her mother, Amelia. She didn't want to see her daughter raising a child without a father, someone she'd never even met! And Julie cruelly continued to remind Caitlin that she'd made a terrible mess of everything by getting married in secret and not telling them about James from the beginning.

In time, Caitlin had to stop working because of her pregnancy, which to her was her biggest blessing and the only thing that about her situation that gave her any joy. And now that she had time, she began looking into James's pension benefits.

Caitlin maintained her closeness to her family and stayed involved with their lives. But Amelia wasn't acting the same way towards her so she decided to talk to Julie about it.

She explained that their mother was treating her differently than before and that she didn't know why.

"You don't know why?! Are you kidding me?" Julie shouted. "What do you expect her to do, Caitlin? You've lied to the entire family!"

"Well, I'm already twenty-one. And that was the first time I was intimate with anyone. I thought that mother, of all people, would surely understand that I haven't been with anyone before my marriage! And honestly, Julie, I really didn't like hiding it.

But we were married the morning before we spent our first night together if you really want to know the truth!"

"Then why did you hide getting married in the first place, Caitlin?" Julie demanded.

"I was so embarrassed because I wasn't as mature or grown up as you and my sisters, who looked forward to getting married. I should've known about these dreams, shouldn't I? So, I freed myself to grow up like the rest of the girls. Even girlfriends when I was in high school used to talk all the time about being romantic and getting married. So I wanted to do the right thing, and so did James. He'd never been with a woman before! We were so much alike. We really were made for each other," Caitlin sobbed.

"You want to know something, Caitlin? Don't feel so backward or embarrassed. I'm older than you and I feel the same way."

"Really, you do, Julie?"

"Really, Caitlin."

"How's that, Julie, when you say you're getting married to Anthony, and you're really looking forward to moving in with him before the wedding? You're being a hypocrite, then, for criticizing me. After all, I was married first!"

"Yes, but I'm getting married because I know Anthony is successful and will take excellent care of me, Caitlin! Anthony's so kind and generous that he even asked our brother Timothy to move in with us so he can help him with finances while he's learning to be a mason," Julie said.

"Oh, that's so wonderful, Julie! Anthony's going to make an excellent husband, and I'm so happy for both of you, and for Timothy! But still, if you're not ready for intimacy, and you're moving in with him now, then why aren't you getting married first? And what are you going to do when temptation strikes, like when I was overwhelmed?" Caitlin asked.

"I don't really know, because I haven't planned on doing anything else with my life, other than making a lot of money and helping the family! Maybe it's because I'm almost twenty-three and I want a big wedding. I don't want to be an old maid. I want to be married for the same reasons you did. For love," Julie told her.

"What about love, Julie?" Caitlin asked.

Julie explained. "Remember when we were younger, and you didn't like to talk about romance because it bothered you so much?"

"Yes, I do!" Caitlin exclaimed.

"Why did it bother you so much?" Julie asked.

Caitlin said, "I always felt that it was wrong and that it was too personal to be discussed. Not that I didn't love James, because I loved him dearly. But I always felt that there was something more that I didn't understand. Then, before being intimate with James, I trembled so much. And this bothered me even more, because I'd heard romance is supposed to be so enchanting!"

"So I poured my heart out to James. And I got the biggest surprise of my life when he understood the problem!"

Caitlin went on to tell Julie about her conversation with James during their weekend together in Maryland before he died.

"James answered my cry, Julie!"

He told me, "I think I know why you're still feeling that something between us is wrong or missing, Caitlin! It's because we're not married!"

"I then asked him, "Do you really think that my anxiety or emptiness is from not being married? How does that make any sense?"

"James answered me by saying, "Yes, I believe it's marriage that's missing, because I think that something happens mystically by consenting to marry each other, Caitlin!"

"Then James explained about commitment and dedication, and about being made for each other. He then asked me the most beautiful question a woman in love wants to hear," Caitlin said.

"James said, "Why don't we get married first and make this right, Caitlin? Because, in all honesty, I'll always feel this emptiness, too, otherwise!"

"So, now you know, Julie. That's exactly what James said to me, word for word!"

Caitlin continued: "So, between visiting the new air base and picking out a dress for your wedding,

One of Seventeen

James and I went to get our blood tests and then we went straight to a little chapel where we were married. But, Julie, it ended much too soon! I'll never know the serenity of a truer love than James's tender words playing over and again in my head!"

"Wow," Julie told her sister. "It sounds like a beautiful, magical romance that ended far too soon!"

"And I think you and I might both have the same intimacy problem, but for different reasons," Julie told her.

Caitlin asked, "Different reasons? Do you think it's partly because we were abandoned when we were so young, and instead of feeling hurt or even sad, we buried it with gratitude to our parents and never gave our own feelings a second thought?"

"That sounds like it to a certain extent," said Julie. But I also think our parents are still living in the 1940s, or even worse, like in 1917, when they were born. I think they were too strict raising us. Of course, it was out of love that they overprotected us."

"Maybe it was effective after all," Caitlin exclaimed. I think my feelings of romantic passion towards men were numb long before I met James, but thankfully yours haven't, Julie!"

"Maybe this is what happened to our parents, Caitlin said. "When our natural father left us, our mother might've been so heartbroken about having to take care of so many of us by herself.

It must have been so hard for her to bear without outside help! Just think about her misfortune. Our poor mother was deeply in love, then betrayed, and then abandoned while she was pregnant. No wonder she died giving birth to Stacey!"

Caitlin continued. "You know something else, Julie? I think I've been holding a grudge towards men since I was six-years-old, and it's only now shown its ugly head.

Julie shook her head and sighed, "You sound very much like romantic love intrigues you, Caitlin! So, what are you going to do about this observation, now that you're having a baby?" Julie asked.

Caitlin said, "James understood that I had anxieties about romance and intimacy. And he was so kind and patient with me. We got over our uneasiness by marrying first and making things right. I believe that everything works out when we create bonds with those around us, whatever way we come to it. James never betrayed or deserted me. I never felt the kind of contempt that our mother and so many others have had to suffer!"

"Did you love James?" Julie asked.

"I loved him more than I've ever loved anyone," Caitlin told her. "I still trust his way of loving."

"Caitlin," Julie asked. "Will you please forgive me for being so cold and callous to you? I never should have said that you disgraced the Eden family by getting married in secret and for not telling us about James."

Caitlin laughed and said, "Sure, I forgive you, Julie. You're my favorite sister. But what on earth ever made you so bossy to me all the time?"

"It's because I've envied you for my entire life, Caitlin. Your grades were always better than mine and you were on the Student Council. You were fearless in all your adventures, and you never expected a man to take care of you! It was also your way of always doing everything to please people. I looked at that as a weakness, as you were buying your friendships. And when I rose above you by working overtime and making more money, everyone around us admired me more than you! But they were wrong. They should have seen your confidence that came from all the love you have inside you."

"Oh, Julie, my own brokenness flooded my heart and I cared for all brothers and sisters, all who had been abandoned. Before James, there wasn't any room left for a man! Who would have thought my misery about working on Sundays would have turned out to be the best job in the world, where I met the best man in the world? Because I listened to you, it led me to James! But now I've lost the perfect love who completed me in every way. And that one brief romantic experience makes me want to keep all people, men, women, and children, from ever feeling such deep loneliness or despair ever again. I want them all to know the power of being loved and cherished!"

She went on. "Julie, it seems to be true though, that we're all really like Adam and Eve in some ways. But instead of covering our nakedness with fig leaves, we're trying to cover our true feelings by not discussing them. Do you think something is trying to nudge us in the right direction by using anxiety? Maybe it's pointing us to a better life. I want to find out if this is true."

Caitlin said. "I'm just thinking about how overwhelmed with romantic love people are today so that they overlook any of the consequences of their actions. I worry about how it's going to affect the younger generation. It really breaks my heart to think that my child will have to go through life not knowing the enhancement of true romance. Our parents' old-fashioned ideas are becoming extinct. But we need to learn from them and keep them in mind because they seem to work better. It bothers me hearing people mock their ideas. Truth is never outdated. Their stories should be the ones we tell our children."

"Oh, Caitlin, you're driving me insane and you're talking too much!" Julie said. "Why are you always trying to find answers to impossible questions? It's not our place, and it's a mystery for us all?"

"I think you're right," sighed Caitlin.

One of Seventeen

"I'm so grateful that James came into my life, even though it was so short. He explained men's anxiety about romance and intimacy, and how they're biologically different from us, even though in some ways we're more complicated and sensitive than men. But women can help men by not tempting a man's weakness when it comes to intimacy. I believe James was an angel sent to teach this to me so I can pass it along. He even used to talk to me about using his prosperity to adopt as many children as he could. He wanted to give them a home and teach them the value and security of having a solid family."

"I'm not sorry for being intimate with James. I'm just sorry that I haven't been able to explain it clearly enough. It's been bothering me for my entire life that I didn't know how to talk about my feelings. James was the angel who got through to me. Can't you see now, Julie, that I never dreamed of or even expected a man to take care of me? But even now, James is taking care of me and the baby with his life insurance. He knew I wanted to help take care of everyone in our family. He covered everything by committing himself to marriage and claiming me as his wife. That's what'll give our baby his name. And I need to pass this knowledge along."

Julie sighed and said, "Caitlin, I appreciate your ideas, your honesty about your experiences, and of not expecting too much from others. But enough of

Catherine Nagle

that for now. We need to get back to making plans for my wedding and for your baby shower, now that I've decided to push up my wedding date and be married before I move in with my guy!"

6

Along Comes Sweet Noelle

Julie and Anthony's wedding were the next big celebration for the Eden family. Everyone busily prepared for the wedding and the birth of Caitlin's baby. Caitlin hadn't gained much weight yet, so she was able to wear the dress she'd bought in Maryland with James to Julie's wedding.

She was thrilled to be helping Julie and Anthony get their apartment ready by shopping for their household linens and décor. To Caitlin's surprise, Julie gave her a beautiful baby shower the month following her wedding. Caitlin received all the gifts she needed from the Marino family and her Eden siblings.

Julie's wedding and Caitlin's baby's shower were wonderful celebrations and the unions of three families. And the next big surprise was Julie's announcement of her own pregnancy at Caitlin's shower.

Then, shortly after the shower, sweet Noelle was born at seven pounds, one ounce. Fortunately, Amelia helped teach her daughter everything she needed to know about taking care of a newborn. Even Carmen, her father, put in his two cents. Everyone adored little Noelle and wanted to be a part of her life. This made Caitlin happy and she appreciated all the extra help she got from the rest of the family. Soon Noelle turned into a toddler, ready to explore the world by taking her first step.

One day, Caitlin decided to take Stacey and Timothy to the beach with Noelle because they wanted to spend time with the little one. Amelia agreed and warned her to be careful driving, and to put sunblock and a hat on Noelle so she wouldn't get sunburned. Caitlin said that it was going to be a perfect beach day, and that she didn't mind driving in the daytime. They'd stop halfway for lunch so she'd have a break.

Amelia asked if they'd stop over at James's parents' summer house, since they'd be nearby, but Caitlin said they wouldn't have enough time. She planned to take Noelle for the whole week over the fourth of July, and the Marinos were looking forward to it. Her in-laws gave Noelle anything she wanted since she was their first granddaughter. Caitlin didn't want her little girl getting too spoiled because she was so sweet and didn't want her turning into a brat. Still, she was grateful for the Marinos' generosity. She knew how much they loved James and missed him.

Caitlin kept in touch with James family, especially for Noelle's sake. The Marinos hadn't known about Caitlin and that James had married her, and didn't know about her pregnancy until after James died. They were overwhelmed and glad when they learned that James had left them with a pregnant daughter-in-law. And they cherished their beautiful little granddaughter.

Caitlin said she hoped Stacey and Timothy would have fun at the beach because they both seem so lost with everyone moving out of the house. She knew Timothy missed everyone since he'd moved in with Julie and Anthony. But she knew Anthony was helping him pay for trade school, and Timothy repaid him and Julie by helping take care of their little girl, Arianna.

Amelia was glad, too. She and Carmen were grateful for all they were doing for Timothy. And they were happy to see him being so loving and protective of Arianna. But she told Caitlin that the house was emptying out too quickly for her and Carmen and that they were happy to still have her and Noelle, and Stacey for a little while longer. Amelia said the three girls kept her and Carmen on their toes and that they didn't know what they'd do without them.

Amelia admitted to Caitlin that Noelle was her favorite. She said that everyone knew and felt it was only right because she didn't have a father. She believed they all understood that every child needs both parents. Amelia knew it wasn't always the norm and felt lucky that she and Carmen were able to give their kids two parents. She also felt lucky that the family hadn't had any sicknesses or deaths like other families, aside from losing

James. She and Carmen wished they'd known him better, but they did have Noelle, who was a gift to all of them. Amelia told Caitlin that she believed children needed their mothers the most, and Noelle was lucky to have her. She reminded Caitlin that Carmen wasn't always around when she was growing up because of his work. But they had plenty of money, the same way Caitlin now did, thanks to James. Having money made it easier and because the Edens were financially secure, Amelia had been able to raise her children without any interference, the same as when Amelia's aunt took her in and raised her.

Caitlin said she'd never want to forget the love Amelia and Carmen gave them and that she hopes to pass that love along to Noelle.

Amelia thanked her and told Caitlin that she knew how much love all of her children gave her and Carmen in return.

Then they stopped talking so they could get going to the shore while the sun was still out and so that Noelle wouldn't be out after dark, breathing in the night air, something that worried Amelia.

Promising to be home before dark, Caitlin backed out of the driveway.

Before long, they arrived at the shore. Timothy and Stacey helped carry all their things to the beach, while Caitlin pushed Noelle in a stroller. Caitlin brought a playpen for her, along with plastic buckets and shovels to make sandcastles. Noelle enjoyed looking at the sandcastles, but she was still too young to run around on her own. Besides, the sand was too hot for her to walk on, so she stayed on the blanket and under the beach umbrella. Her aunt and uncle bought her a snow cone to help her cool off, and they laughed watching her sip it, dip her fingers into it, and then lick it off!

Later that day, when they got back home, they were full of stories for the rest of the family. Everyone was interested in hearing about how Noelle enjoyed her first time at the beach. She was always the center of attraction in the Eden household. But it was already late, so Caitlin took her upstairs for her bath and put her to bed. Then she came back down to have a cup of tea with her mother. Amelia said that Noelle would sleep well and through the night after being in the fresh ocean air all day, and that they'd have time to talk.

Amelia told Caitlin that their conversation in the morning had been on her mind all day and Caitlin asked why.

She reminded her daughter that she'd said that Noelle was her favorite because she was fatherless, unlike like the rest of her grandchildren. She said that was the reason she and Carman showed her more attention than the others. They felt it was what they were supposed to do. Some people think that if a child is adopted, the parents don't know how to love them.

Catherine Nagle

Amelia said, "I never gave birth, but having raised all seventeen of you is as good as a bloodline for us. My aunt raised me alone and was the first person who showed me what a mother figure should be. Noelle's loss of her father reminds me why I adopted all of you: to fill that void with a mother's love. That's what saved me as a child whose parents died. That's what Aunt Katherine showed me—how to love a child and how to be a mother."

Caitlin asked Amelia how she came to know this. "Was it because you were such a small child when you lost both your parents and you had no siblings to turn to?"

"Some of that was an issue for a while. But my aunt was such a wonderful, loving mother to me. I was always grateful that she took me in and raised me so well. I learned how to trust, and when I grew up and got married, I learned not to be worried, even when your dad was away for weeks at a time on business. But I realize that some men who are unfaithful to their wives."

"I know they are, Mom. And women also cheat. But I know you never looked at another man!"

"You're right, I didn't. I busied myself with taking care of something more important: my children! For me, there's no lasting satisfaction in anything unless it provides our love to those around us, especially to our children! But for every child who is separated from his or her parents, we're all guilty if we don't open our arms to them. As a parent, we have an important role to fill, one we should never forget! Besides, I've had all of you children reminding me to do that, Caitlin!"

"But, Mom, didn't you miss Dad's help and having him around?" Caitlin asked.

"Sure I did, especially during trying times. But there was never a dull moment with all of you around. With Dad away so much, I didn't have to divide my attention and could give more of myself to all of you!"

"What are people supposed to do if they don't have any children or have just one or two?" Caitlin asked. "What do they do with their free time? Will they get in trouble by not having children?"

"Of course not!" Amelia said. "Childless people do things that people *with* children don't have time to do! They become innovators, humanitarians, and philanthropists. They make our world a better place! We need role models like them. They teach us that our happiness is not dependent on what other people bring to us, but rather is something we give to others in whatever way we're able!"

Amelia explained further. "Sometimes people with children and spouses desert them by falling out of love or leaving because they're unhappy. And sometimes they're unfaithful. Or they get carried away by a consuming desire, or greed, and neglect their children. I can only speak for myself, Caitlin! Your father doesn't like to discuss these things with me. That's because over twenty years ago, his brother-in-law, Richard, deserted his wife and daughter, all because of his passion for another woman. His wife was broken by it, and your father could never forgive him! That's why I can't ever bring up the subject of his brother-in-law. I think he just blanks him out of his mind, as if he doesn't exist."

"But you never told us about this, Mom!" Caitlin said. "What about Uncle Richard's wife and little girl? We were always under the impression that Aunt Isabella left Uncle Richard and moved out of the country, to start a new life with Emma. So, what really happened to them? Where are they now? And why on earth doesn't Dad keep in touch with them? Why is this all such a big secret?"

"Caitlin! Please stop asking so many questions! Ask your father to tell you about them. They're his family and he refuses to share the mystery with me. But I'd be very careful if I were you, and I wouldn't bring it up right now! He's too sensitive about it. Just let it go, like I had to do. Trust that the right time will come for him to tell us!"

"Alright, Mom," Caitlin said. "I won't bring it up again until you're both ready to tell us about it. I promise you. But your patience is incredible! You've already waited twenty years believing the right time will come for Dad to explain!"

Then Caitlin asked her mother for advice, in case she wanted to get married again someday. "I have so much respect and trust in your wisdom." Caitlin said.

"You're so young, and without a husband, you need to be careful about a man's qualities and morals if you want to marry again. Remember that you're not supposed to change a man to suit you. That's not your job. And as a mother, your first job is to take care of Noelle before anything else. Then, if you do things right, your heart will open and the right person will show up in your life. But only if you're looking for one."

"I believe you, Mom. That's exactly how James came into my life. I wasn't even thinking of meeting anyone. I just wanted to help the family when I met him. Julie also helped me to see what I had to do, rather than thinking about myself. But right now, I'm perfectly content just the way we are, living here with you, Noelle, and the rest of our family," Caitlin said.

7

Letting Go

While Noelle was a baby, Caitlin had no desire to leave the Eden home. Why would she? Raising Noelle was her whole life, and the little girl had the attention of everyone in the house since the day she was born. That meant Caitlin had all the help she needed with the baby. But when Noelle was four, Caitlin mentioned to Amelia that she wanted to go back to work.

But Amelia didn't agree. She carried on and said, "Be patient, Caitlin! You can go back to work when Noelle starts school next year. Besides, you're a tremendous help to me and I'd miss that if you went to work. And the most important thing is that we really love having you with us.

I'm getting tired and my eyesight is poor. And your father's not as sharp as he used to be. So we depend on you so much. Besides, Stacey will be leaving for the University of Pittsburg soon, and Timothy's finished trade school and will be a skilled marble cutter before long. Soon he'll start working full time at the Edison Stone Quarry. He'll move back home for a little while because his job is closer to us, until he gets his own apartment. Our

One of Seventeen

house is emptying out, and even sweet little Noelle will be off to school next year!"

"I know, Mom. I was wandering through all the empty rooms upstairs when Noelle was napping. I was reminiscing about when we were all so young, without a care in the world, napping just like Noelle," Caitlin said, smiling.

"Mom, remember the time when Noelle and Julie's little girl Arianna accidentally locked themselves in the front bedroom on the third floor? They yelled for help, but no one could hear them. Then they made a flag with one of the pillowcases, wrote S.O.S. on it, and tied it to the end of a wire coat hanger and waved it out the bedroom window! Luckily some of the boys were outside playing basketball and saw the white flag and heard them shouting. I thought that flag was so clever of the girls. We'll tell their kids about it someday. They were only three years old!?"

"Yes," Amelia said. "They were playing going up and down the staircase while we were drinking having tea around the kitchen table. We lost track of time and the girls! Noelle told me she was the clever one who came up with the idea of the flag, and Arianna let her take all the credit. Those two girls are like sisters, always competing with each other since the day they were born. But I believe they'll grow out of it in time."

"Mom, you thought Noelle was so bright because she started talking early. You worried that some talent scout might spot her and take her away from us!" Caitlin said with a laugh. "What on earth made you ever think of that?"

"That's true. I raised all of you children and I haven't seen anyone as bright as Noelle other than you. I thought Noelle might very well be a genius!"

"Really? You thought that about me, Mom?" Caitlin asked surprised. "What did I ever do that was so bright?"

"Remember when you were in the first grade and all the students were asked to share something special about their family? Well, you stood up very proudly and explained that you have sixteen brothers and sisters; nine boys and eight girls. You told them that this is very, very, special because it's the biggest number of children in one family that you'd ever heard! Then you rattled off all their names and ages. Your teacher, Mrs. Boysen, even wrote to me and pointed out your intelligence to me, along with your love for our family!"

"Aww, thank you, Mom, for reminding me about that, and about Mrs. Boysen. She was my favorite teacher! She always made me feel special. I forgot all about that," Caitlin said.

As they sat at the table, there was suddenly a knock at the door. Amelia asked Caitlin to see who it was while she ran upstairs to make herself more presentable."

Caitlin opened the door and asked the gentleman how she could help him.

One of Seventeen

The man told her his name was Michael DiCaprio, a developer with *Up Towne Builders*, and he wanted to talk with her parents.

"I'll get them for you. And what shall I tell them this is about?"

"I want to talk to them about their property. We'd like to make an offer to buy the house and their land," Mr. DiCaprio told her.

"Oh, no! I'm sorry, but you must be mistaken! I don't know how you came up with that idea. I'll get my parents for you, Mr. DiCaprio. But I can assure you that this house is certainly not for sale!"

Caitlin ran upstairs to get her parents and was so astonished that she forgot to even offer Mr. DiCaprio a seat. She was that surprised and upset at the idea of someone buying the house. She told her parents why Michael DiCaprio was there, and noticed her father quietly nodding to her mother.

"Amelia," Carmen said. "Can you please come into the other room with me for a second so we can talk privately before we go downstairs and talk with our visitor?"

After Carmen talked to Amelia for some time, he went downstairs alone.

He introduced himself to Michael and asked him what he wanted to see him about.

"Mr. Eden, I'm very sorry to bring this up, but as you probably know, your property taxes have risen steeply. And we think that you're not in a position to hold onto your estate," Mr. DiCaprio said politely. I'd like to help you by making a most generous offer for your house and land, and by suggesting an exciting venue to move to!"

Carmen told him, "We love our home, Mr. DiCaprio, and I already knew some time ago that it wasn't going to be easy to keep it going after our children, who have helped us financially, moved on to have families of their own. You're right--I've used up all my savings. But I've kept this fact from everyone, even my wife, because I knew that our widowed daughter and our granddaughter depend on this house as their home and foundation. I've been hoping that something good would turn up, and honestly, you just did! So thank you very much, Mr. DiCaprio! And what exactly is this venue you mentioned? I want to have my wife hear about it, too."

Carmen called to Amelia and she came downstairs to join them. After introducing them, Michael DiCaprio told them about his company's proposal.

"We're home builders and developers, and with your estate and the lot down the road, we've already done estimates and drawn up blueprints for luxury townhouses with award-winning designs. We'd like to offer your family another house down the road until the new townhomes are completed next year, and then you can pick the house you like best."

One of Seventeen

After talking things over from every angle, Carmen and Amelia invited Michael to have lunch with them. He was too pressed for time to stay any longer having other appointments to attend. But their conversation was very pleasant, even with the unexpected news.

Before he left, Carmen asked Michael to leave him the paperwork and blueprints so he could go over everything with Amelia and the rest of the family and discuss them. Michael agreed, handed over the papers, said goodbye and left.

Caitlin had been listening at the top of the stairs and had heard everything. She felt terrible that she hadn't known about the huge increase in taxes or that her parents had used up all of their savings. They'd never even hinted about their financial concerns to her, not wanting to burden her. All she knew was that her father received a disability check from the government. It was her parents' way of continuing to protect her as they'd done since she came under their roof as a girl.

Caitlin also received a government pension arranged by James that covered all of her and Noelle's expenses. She contributed the rest of her income for groceries and the Eden family's necessities, which her parents thought was plenty. She didn't spend frivolously and didn't keep extra money in a savings account. Her parents didn't ask her to contribute anything more than she did, knowing how generous she was with them. They were grateful for her sacrifices and help. And they loved having Caitlin and Noelle live with them.

Carmen and Amelia talked for a while before they sat down and told everyone that Michael's offer for the house and property was for a very fair price and they should accept it. He explained everything clearly so they'd understand all the details.

They didn't need such a big house full of empty rooms anymore. Some of them hadn't been used in years. And the grounds would be put to better use as a community of townhouses for more families to live in and enjoy. Carmen and Amelia would move into a townhouse and would still feel like they were home. Caitlin and Noelle would have plenty of space with them, and most important, Noelle could go to the same school, which is where all of the Eden children went.

Amelia immediately agreed with Carmen, and so did everyone else. It was a well-planned transition that pointed to a better future for them.

8

Crying in the Attic

Michael DiCaprio called to set up an appointment to meet the Eden family at the townhouse where they'd be moving, which was just a few blocks away from the location of their soon to-be-built new, custom designed townhouse. When everyone arrived, they were astonished at the spaciousness and beautiful layout of their temporary unit, an older model that was quite up to date compared to their house. Then Michael took them over to see the model townhouse in the new section where they'd eventual live.

They thought the new section of townhouses was designed more for professionals, people without children or who were retired people, which was evident by the layout and built-in features. On the other hand, the older section, where they'd be staying temporarily, had mostly families with children living there, and it featured play areas, jungle gyms and other child-friendly features in their backyards. After comparing the two different sections of townhouses, everyone agreed that the temporary location would be better for little Noelle and if things worked out there, maybe they wouldn't move to the brand-new place. And in the weeks that followed, they eagerly began packing. Caitlin and Amelia were on the job and organizing everything in the house.

Caitlin told Amelia that she'd start packing the things in the upstairs attic first and her mother agreed. She reminded Caitlin to put aside the things they no longer needed so Carmen could drop them off at Goodwill or another charity. She reminded her to label all the boxes they were taking to the new house by room to make it easier for the delivery men. Caitlin asked her mom to keep Noelle occupied downstairs with her so she could concentrate and not get distracted by her little girl. Amelia agreed and said she'd let her know when lunch was ready.

Caitlin started to open the boxes in the attic and sort things, and this brought back so many wonderful memories. She came across a picture of herself and her siblings when she was just six, before they were adopted. She put it aside to surprise Noelle and show her daughter how she'd looked at her age. Then she came across a picture of her four smiling younger brothers, each a year apart and all dressed alike in their Jungle Jim combat suits that Carmen had picked out for them one Christmas.

Then she came to a larger box with her dusty typewriter in it. She cleaned it off and tried typing a few words, but the ribbon was dried out because she hadn't used it in years. She reminisced about typing menus for the restaurant when she was a waitress. But then she suddenly flashed on a quick picture in her mind of typing something different, but she didn't know what it said and the words disappeared. She carefully repacked the typewriter, making sure it wouldn't be damaged during the move, and proudly marked the box with the words, "Caitlin's Typewriter." She cherished it as a new beginning, along with moving into their new home.

Next, she came across another box that was marked "Important Papers." She opened it and began going through them. One was a letter addressed to her father from Uncle Richard, his brother-in-law, with the return address of a Hospital for Mental Health. Caitlin read Richard's letter with great interest. It said:

Dear Carmen,

>   I sure hope you're doing fine. I've heard from a friend that you're still working for the Yale Rail Line and that you bought a big estate. He said that you work day and night and keep long hours on the job, so I'm really concerned about you.
>
>   I hope someday you'll forgive me for what happened to our family. It wasn't all my fault that they died

Catherine Nagle

in the Influenza outbreak. I know I was no angel, but you shouldn't blame me for their deaths.

Please write me back! You're the only family I have left.

I really hope to hear from you.

Sincerely,
Richard

Caitlin tried to read the date on the postmark, but it was worn off the tattered envelope. Uncle Richard must have written it to her father before he was married because there was no mention of Amelia or the children. She wondered if her mother knew about that letter, or if her father had kept it from her. She couldn't believe her father could be so cold-hearted and unforgiving to his brother-in-law. Normally he was so loving, accepting and understanding toward everyone. What could Richard have done that was so unforgivable? She didn't want to show the letter to her mother because her mom had told her to let it go and not mention Richard to Carmen to avoid a conflict. So Caitlin kept her promise to her mother. But she took the letter with her and hid it, hoping that someday the time would come when her father would be ready to talk about Richard.

Later, when Amelia called Caitlin to come down to have lunch, Caitlin quickly closed the box of

One of Seventeen

papers, intending to look through it again later. She went to her room to hide the letter, tucking it inside one of her favorite books.

Amelia called to her again, saying that Noelle was asking for her and getting fidgety because it was almost time for her afternoon nap.

Her mother never gave up lecturing Caitlin about her responsibilities as a mother and reminding her that Noelle needing a nap, even once she was four. It was something she'd done with all of her children, and she believed that napping was as necessary as eating, drinking, and playing outside in the fresh air.

After putting the letter away, Caitlin hurried downstairs to have lunch. Then she asked Noelle for a hug, saying she'd missed her. She asked what she and Amelia were doing all morning while she was busy sorting and packing.

Her little girl giggled and said they'd played hide-and-seek, and that Pop-Pop had pointed out where Mom-Mom was hiding.

"He did?" Caitlin said with a laugh. "Well, the next time he has his turn at hiding and thinks he's safe, Mom-Mom will make sure to point him out for you!" Then they all laughed!

After lunch, Caitlin brought Noelle upstairs for her nap. Then she lay down next to her and read her a story, and soon the little girl fell asleep.

Caitlin was eager to get back up to the attic and read more of those important papers in the box.

Catherine Nagle

After all, she'd agreed to help sort things out! But then she found another letter, this one addressed to her father's sister, her Aunt Isabella, who was Uncle Richard's wife. It was from a woman named Susan.

After she read the letter, she wished she'd never known about it because now she'd have to keep secret what she'd found out and not let her father know. She might even keep it from her mother, who didn't seem to know anything about this mystery, either. The letter from Susan to Aunt Isabella read as follows:

> Dear Isabella,
>
> I'm sorry to have to tell you this, but as you already know, Richard and I are in love. He wants to divorce you and marry me. He also wants me to raise little Emma because he says that you're not mentally fit to raise her and this worries him.
>
> He's already moved half of my belongings into your summer house at the beach. We've been seeing each other ever since the day you called him to tell him that you were pregnant, when you thought he was away on a business trip. But he was right beside me the

One of Seventeen

whole time you were talking, and I overheard the entire conversation. You always believed that he was away on business. But the truth is, he was always with me instead. He just told you that to keep you from knowing the truth.

I want you to know that Richard's bought me diamond earrings and takes me shopping at the finest stores right outside of town. Richard buys me anything I want. He's already met my entire family, and they, too, have often stayed at your beach house on the weekends, including one entire summer. That was the summer you didn't come to the beach house because you were pregnant with little Emma. When we were there, Richard always took us all out on his boat!

He didn't want to leave you until after the baby was born. So, he waited. And then waited even longer, until she was a toddler. Now he says he's waited long enough. He hopes you'll give him a divorce and custody of little Emma because he wants me to be her mother.

Catherine Nagle

He's willing to offer you a lot of money to go away and make a new life for yourself. He loves <u>me</u>, Isabella, not you! He told me that he realizes now that he never really loved you in the first place. He says that now that he's met me, he knows what true love is.

Please do the right thing and let him go.

Susan

Caitlin couldn't believe what she'd just read. The letter upset her terribly and made her cry. She couldn't imagine what poor Isabella must have felt when she read it! Now she understood her father's silence and unforgiving attitude towards Richard.

Caitlin couldn't make sense of the two letters together. She wondered what Richard meant in his letter when he apologized to her father and said that it wasn't his fault that they died in the Influenza outbreak. That remark confused her. And because her father never talked about his family, not even to her mother, it was a mystery to all of them.

Caitlin's mother interrupted her tears by calling to her again to come downstairs. She didn't know the secrets her daughter had just discovered in those letters in the attic. She told her mother she'd be right down and had more than enough packing for the day.

Caitlin composed herself and rushed back downstairs to her bedroom, where she tucked Isabella's letter into her book with Richard's letter, then she went down to the kitchen. When she saw her mother, she noticed that she'd been crying too. But when she asked Amelia, she said her tears were over sentimental feelings about moving out of their home.

She tried to hide her sadness by immediately changing the subject, saying they'd have to ask Carmen to start taking more of these boxes to his charities. They needed to get everything packed and out before the contractors came to knock down the old house.

Caitlin said she'd get back to sorting again early the next morning and that she was almost through sorting everything in the boxes.

Caitlin helped her mother get dinner ready while Stacey played with Noelle and her dollhouse. Her mind was racing, trying to figure out where Isabella and Emma were living now. She didn't want to stir anything up about the letters she discovered, so she kept everything to herself. After reading Susan's letter, Caitlin believed that Isabella was hiding from Richard because he wanted to take little Emma away. She had heartbreaking visions of a child being separated from her mother and the idea took Caitlin's breath away. She believed that her father knew exactly where her Aunt Isabella and cousin Emma were living, and that he'd kept it secret from his wife and kids to protect his sister and niece!

But she didn't want to say anything to further upset Amelia after seeing the sadness on her face over moving out of their house. She knew that her mother was trying to hide her real feelings about it from everyone, so Caitlin tried to be cheerful all through dinner. She talked excitedly about all the packing she was getting done and that she'd cleared out the whole attic. She added that she was eager to start on Noelle's and her own bedrooms next, unless Amelia wanted her to do something else first.

Amelia agreed and added that Stacey had already finished her own packing since she'd started long before and was eager to move on. She told Caitlin that she and Carmen were all packed, too, since everything they owned fit into one box between them.

Amelia and Carmen didn't have much to pack because they never bought clothes unless they absolutely needed them. They owned just what they needed and nothing more, and they'd never changed this habit, even when they were very well off.

After dinner, Amelia asked Caitlin to help pack up the kitchen things next. Caitlin agreed, then asked when they'd move into the townhouse.

One of Seventeen

She was surprised to find out that the moving trucks would arrive early the next day and that they'd take turns watching Noelle so she wouldn't get hurt or be in the way. She added with a sigh that they wouldn't have to clean the house since it would be torn down.

❧

The following morning, the movers took everything out of the house. There weren't many boxes because most of the kids had already moved out.

Caitlin again stopped herself from thinking about the letters, but they continued to haunt her. She shed some tears, too, about leaving the Eden house. She focused on moving forward, trying in vain to find words of comfort and promises for the future as she roamed the empty bedrooms, where traces remained on the walls where pictures and awards once hung. She reminisced about her brothers playing ball, hockey, and even basketball in their bedrooms at night, startling the whole family, especially the girls. They'd sure made a lot of noise scrimmaging and bouncing balls off their walls.

Caitlin again stopped herself from thinking about the letters, and suddenly noticed something sparkling on the floor. It was an old glittered swim cap strap laying on one of the girls' empty bedroom floors. She picked it up and ran her fingers along the textures of hardened glue and glitter of the strap that she hand-made for a special show. It had been hers and it brought back all sorts of memories. The sparkles reminded Caitlin that she'd belonged to something bigger than herself, just as her family did.

9

Uptown

The townhouse they moved into was very different from the massive Eden estate they'd been so accustomed to for all those years. But their new home had every possible luxury, especially compared to their old house, which had become so outdated. The townhouse was made of beautiful red brick and had an attached garage. Carmen loved going into the house that way and considered it a luxury. He was impressed with all the latest gadgets that he and his sons enjoyed playing with to learn how they worked. Everyone was grateful that Chas and Luke, the engineering students, were still around to show them how their new, upgraded appliances and other standard equipment worked. The boys were proud to be able to show their mother how to use the new remote controls for the television, thermostat, stove, ceiling fans, window treatments, and even the refrigerator settings. They were all fascinated with the latest technologies in their new house!

Carmen asked Amelia how she liked her new kitchen and she admitted that she just loved it. There were so many practical features than what she'd been used to, but she knew she'd modernize very quickly, and laughed.

Next Carmen asked Caitlin if she liked her new room with the adjoining door leading to Noelle's room and said he thought she'd love it.

She told him it was perfect in every way for both of them. She said she liked other features of the house, especially the sliding doors from the kitchen to the huge deck because it was so private, with all the shrubs and trees. She also was happy about the spacious backyard for Noelle to play in and the jungle gym that she could get to from the deck. She said the house had everything they could want and Carmen agreed.

That's when Amelia told Carmen that she was so content with everything that they might be better off just staying in there instead of moving again into the brand-new townhouse that was being built for them. She thought that the current townhouse was new enough for them after living in the old 1900s estate. And she liked that it was still close to everything, especially Noelle's school, which actually was even closer now.

Carmen agreed with his wife but suggested they wait until they'd had a chance to settled in. They'd take a drive around the neighborhood before deciding after they lived in the house for a while. Then, if they still wanted to stay, they'd talk with Michael DiCaprio about the change of plans.

One of Seventeen

Later that day, Caitlin was up in her new bedroom, finishing up her unpacking when she came across the box that held the key to her house in Maryland and her marriage license. She held the key tight and close to her heart, hearing James's voice in her mind. His sweet, loving words were so unlike the unhappy things she'd read in Susan's letter to Isabella. She decided to put Susan's and Uncle Richard's letters together with her marriage license in her favorite book and put it on her shelf.

After she finished sorting her things, Caitlin went into Noelle's room to put away her new school clothes. As she took them out of the shopping bags and put them on hangers, it reminded her of shopping for her brothers and sisters when they were children.

She looked around Noelle's room and saw that everything was in place so that she'd be ready to start school. Satisfied, she wrote a note to herself to pick up a school bag, books, and pencils for Noelle. Then she went back downstairs to go on an errand.

She told Amelia she was taking Noelle for a haircut and to get school supplies, and her mom reminded her to have Noelle's bangs cut so they'd stay out of her eyes. Caitlin laughed and agreed with her, and said she'd send her best wishes to everyone at the salon.

After the haircut, Caitlin and Noelle went shopping together for her first school bag. Noelle carried it over her shoulders all the way home and into the house, she was so happy with it. When they got home, everyone admired Noelle's pretty new haircut.

Caitlin reminded Amelia of the time when she was six that she tried to cut her own bangs because they were curling up and annoying her. Then she told Noelle about the picture she'd found of herself and her ridiculous cut-off bangs that she'd found in the attic when she was sorting and packing. She told Noell she was around her age when that picture was taken, and that she'd find it and will show it to her.

10
The Truth, Sad Story of Uncle Richard

The next day Amelia asked Caitlin if she'd seen her Carmen, who'd left early that morning to drop off more donations. She wondered if he'd gone to tell Michael DiCaprio that they'd decided not to move again. Caitlin said she hadn't seen him all day and asked if she should call Michael and find out if he'd been there. Amelia agreed, saying that way they wouldn't worry and noted that Carmen never went out for the entire day without letting her know.

When Caitlin called Michael, she found out that her father had come in to tell him the good news about staying in the townhouse. Michael said he was glad they'd made that choice, which would also save him a lot of money. She asked him if her father mentioned going anywhere else, and Michael told her no, not that Carmen had told him. Then Caitlin explained all of this to her mother when she was off the phone. Amelia said she didn't like it and that if he wasn't back by dinner time, she'd have to call someone for help.

But they needn't have worried because shortly after five o'clock, Carmen walked in, followed to everyone's surprise by his long-lost brother-in-law, Richard!

He said, "Amelia, "I'm so sorry, that I didn't call you or let you know I'd be gone all day, but I hadn't planned on it. After going to see Michael DiCaprio's to straighten things out about our decision to stay here, I decided to see how far things had gotten at the old house. I was surprised that the construction crew was only just starting the demolition when I pulled up. But since they knew who I was, they allowed me to stay and watch, as long as I put on protective glasses and a hard hat. Honestly, I can't say that it was easy for me to watch, but I still felt good about the decision we've made for our estate."

Carmen continued, "But then, to my shock, I saw Richard standing beside me! He said he'd looked me up and found my address, and just in the nick of time, found that our estate was still here. Otherwise he'd have had a harder time trying to find me. He'd waited there all morning, hoping to see me. And after the contractors found out that Ricard was my brother-in-law, the demolition team gave him a hard hat and protective glasses to put on, too."

"Richard came back to explain about the tragedy that separated us so many years ago, and I'm so glad that we got together! We had lunch and talked for hours. So now I'm going to explain everything when we all can sit down and listen."

One of Seventeen

Caitlin asked for a few minutes to put on a children's TV show for Noelle, to occupy her in the new family room. Then she quietly sat down next to her mother in the living room and listened to her father tell the story of Uncle Richard. She listened attentively to every word and never mentioned the letters while her father told them Richard's heart-wrenching story:

"I'm sorry that I've never opened up to you about my family's past and the tragic details of the deaths of my nineteen-year-old sister, Isabella and my two-year-old niece, Emma, who was named after my mother. On top of those sorrows, my mother died a couple weeks later. Richard, who was Isabella's husband, came to see me today to ask me to forgive him. But when I finally heard his side of the story after all these years, I'm the one who should be asking him to forgive me!"

"Richard has just been released from a mental health facility, where he's been living for the past twenty years, all because he couldn't forgive himself for getting tangled up with a woman named Susan. He'd also been drinking too much at that time and it led to him landing at that hospital. He's fine now and safe to be on his own, and he'd never harm himself or anyone else. The tragedy began while he was married to my sister, Isabella, who I adored."

"Unfortunately, one day after work, Richard met a beautiful woman named Susan at a cocktail bar.

Susan was very attracted to him and it was hard for an intoxicated Richard to ignore her beauty. She threw herself at him and he fell for her, and she became his mistress. That his better judgement was clouded that he eventually deserted Isabella and little Emma and asked for a divorce."

"Isabella was so heartbroken, and when little Emma came down with Influenza, Isabella, who was taking care of her, was stricken with it, too. They died within days of each another. My mother and I were at the funeral together. The two caskets were buried side by side. It was such a heart-wrenching sight that my mother and I fell into the deepest despair, watching them being lowered into their graves. When they died, nobody knew that my aging mother wasn't in good health after taking care of Isabella and little Emma. To my great sorrow and shock, she, too, died a few weeks later."

"Now I had no family left because my father died of a heart attack when I was only twelve. Isabella and I grew up close after he died, and although we were without a father, we did have a wonderful mother who did everything for us."

"The first thing Richard did when he was released from the hospital was to come and tell me how sorry he was about what he'd done to Isabella by having the affair with Susan. He said that he could never love anyone ever again. But the truth is that he came to his senses and had left Susan. He was going to ask Isabella to forgive him and take him back, but by then, little Emma was already stricken with Influenza and their house was quarantined. For that reason, they wouldn't let him see his wife or child. After Susan found out that Richard wasn't coming back to her, and that he'd gone home to his wife and daughter, she wrote a letter to Isabella that broke her heart. Susan hoped that when Isabella read the letter, she wouldn't take Richard back. That letter was Susan's way of getting revenge. After Isabella and Emma died, I found the letter in Isabella's bureau and showed it to Richard, believing it was true. After Richard saw what Susan had written to Isabella because I showed it to him, he fell into a deep depression and has been in the hospital ever since. That's why I should be asking forgiveness, not Richard," Carmen said.

Amelia, Caitlin, and Richard were in a serious and somber mood after Carmen's sad story. It was hard for them to imagine the sorrow that Carmen and Richard had carried with them for so many years without telling anyone. It was an important lesson for Caitlin and made her realize how important it was to step back and see the whole picture before ever judging anyone else's mistakes. After hearing the real story behind the letters to her father and Isabella that she'd found, Caitlin's sorrow turned to empathy and compassion for her Uncle Richard and a greater understanding of her father.

Everyone was now very quiet as they sat in the living room until Noelle skipped cheerfully back to them and asked if she could come in and sit with the grown-ups. Caitlin said yes and smiled at her little girl.

"Are all the grownups finished talking with Pop-Pop now?" Noelle asked. "And who is Pop-Pop's new friend?"

"He's your Great Uncle Richard, Noelle! Come over here and meet him," Carmen told his granddaughter.

"Is he going to live with us, Pop-Pop? Because I really like him and he has a nice face!" Noelle announced.

"If he wants to live with us, that's perfectly fine with me, Carmen said happily. "And I don't think Mom-Mom would have it any other way!"

And of course Amelia was delighted to have a new addition to her family once again. She said, "Richard, we have an extra bedroom, and we'd love to have you live with us, that is if you have no other plans."

Richard was thrilled. He thanked Amelia and said, "No, I don't have any other plans. But I don't want to inconvenience anyone, either. I came to ask Carmen for forgiveness, and I believe we both understand the whole situation now. I'm also glad that everyone finally heard the truth about what happened to us."

One of Seventeen

"We do understand, Richard, and we're all very sorry for what you've been through," Amelia told him. "You're our family, and there's nothing inconvenient about opening our home to you!" Amelia told him with a gentle smile.

"Come on, Richard, please stay with us and at least give it a try!" Carmen said, his face shining with hope. "If you don't feel comfortable after trying it, you can always leave."

"Thank you!" Richard said. "I really would like that. I just have to get some of my things from the hospital."

Carmen said, "How about we go together and get them right now? I'll drive!" Richard agreed and they left together.

Once they were gone, Caitlin told her mother that she was going upstairs to get the room ready for Uncle Richard. She was thrilled that her parents had offered him a place to live because he'd looked lost and his skin was pale and sallow. She thought that by coming to live with them, they could give Richard comfort and a place to belong so she was glad that he was going to try it. She thought about the letter he'd sent to her father, saying that her dad was the only family Richard had left, and she was happy that Richard would now have all the Edens as his family. And she felt glad to be part of his life.

Meanwhile, as the weeks passed in their new home, Caitlin was fascinated living in the townhouse. She felt like she was in another world!

Catherine Nagle

She's never lived so close to so many people outside the family. They'd never even had any neighbors back at the old estate because it was so private and away from other houses, and surrounded by acres of trees. By contrast, the townhouses were full of families, with neighbors on either side of them and across the street. The neighborhood was close-knit and friendly, with many young children just like Noelle. The school bus made a stop right at her corner, and Noelle would be taking it eventually when she was a little older.

Caitlin noticed that in her new neighborhood, the families had both parents working at demanding and prestigious jobs, but was happy to see that they shared equally the responsibilities of taking care of the children and doing housework. After seeing a lifetime of broken families, orphans, and widows, this glimpse into a different kind of life in the townhouses helped keep Caitlin's dreams for the future alive. She believed that what united people and kept them together was more about belonging than blood. It was something she hoped to teach to Noelle most of all.

11

Settling the Unrest

As she began setting up her new room, Caitlin unpacked her typewriter and put it on the built-in corner desk in her bedroom. She carefully cleaned it and replaced the old ribbon. Then she put in a new sheet of paper and began to type. She wanted to write a story, but she didn't know where to begin, so she didn't end up typing anything. Instead, she played around with words, tossing them around in her head, waiting to see how they sounded.

She thought again about Susan's letter to Isabella, and how she must have felt with those words piercing straight through her heart. She thought about her one-time night of wedded romance with James, and how she still could hear his calming words of serenity that brought peace to her heart and mind. They'd all been much too young to die. And Caitlin believed that the deaths of James, Isabella, and Emma could tell a greater story, and one that would touch people's hearts. But she couldn't write it because didn't know the words. She realized she'd have to come back to the story at some other time, once she'd figured out what they had to say to her. She'd need to listen closely to her heart, be more patient, and trust time.

Suddenly she heard Carmen announce that they'd returned as he and Richard walked into the house with Richard's suitcase. Caitlin called to her father and said to come upstairs and bring Uncle Richards's suitcase. She said that his room was ready, and she'd love to show him around.

Caitlin felt so sorry for her Uncle Richard after she learned about what he'd been through. She couldn't imagine the pain he must've felt for his wife and daughter after reading Susan's letter and then dwelling on it for all those years. Caitlin decided to treat him like a young man still in his twenties because she believed that was his age when his heart, mind, and spirit had stood frozen in time, just as hers had done when James died. She understood her uncle better than anyone else, having also lost her own great love at such a young age.

"Uncle Richard," Caitlin said gently, "You can put your things in this dresser and bureau, and you also have this enormous walk-in-closet for the things that need to be on hangers. It's large enough to be a small bedroom!" she said with a laugh. "And the first door down the hall is your own private bathroom. You can leave your things out on the vanity if you like, since that bathroom is all yours!"

"Thank you so much!" Uncle Richard said. "This is wonderful! You're so kind, Caitlin. Would it be alright if I go back downstairs for a glass of milk and take my pill before going to bed? It helps me sleep."

"Of course, Uncle Richard! You don't have to ask! I'm so glad you're with us. You can do whatever you need to be healthy. Do you just take your pill at night?" Caitlin asked.

"Yes," he told her. "I used to take medication during the day, but now that I've been in therapy, I don't need it anymore. My night-time pill is a natural vitamin supplement, a gentle relaxer to help me sleep. And I don't ever drink alcohol anymore. It just doesn't work for me."

Caitlin said she knew he wasn't much of a drinker, and Uncle Richard told her that stopping at that cocktail bar and having more than a few drinks after work each day was how he'd met Susan, which had led him down the wrong path away from his wife and child. "That's the hardest lesson I've learned about alcohol," Uncle Richard told her. "It's important never to be that vulnerable again. So I stay away from drinking alcohol altogether."

"That's understandable, Uncle Richard!" Caitlin said. "Now that you've told me about your experience with drinking, it's easier for me to understand why there's never been any alcohol in our house! And it explains why our parents have been so strict in warning us about avoiding alcohol! It all makes sense now. That's why our parents don't drink anything but lemonade or water, and only gave us milk," Caitlin told him with a kind smile. "I guess they want to stay alert after they both had terrible tragedies that involved intoxication."

"Yes, Caitlin, they raised you that way for very good reasons," Richard said.

"I'd like to raise Noelle the same way, Uncle Richard, but how do I do that, with all the temptations around her?" Caitlin asked. "I don't think there's any real harm in having an occasional drink, do you?"

"No, Caitlin." He said. "There's no real harm. You just live by those rules about being careful around alcohol and hope your children trust your advice and judgment," Uncle Richard said. Then he smiled warmly at his niece.

"Who knows? Maybe if I'd had a drink at the end of the day with my family, instead of in some bar, that terrible mess wouldn't have happened. But I thought I could control myself," Richard said quietly. "I'll tell you one thing, though. A cocktail bar is no place for a married man with children to be hanging out in, Caitlin! Some men are weak in the presence of a beautiful woman to begin with, and if you add alcohol, it makes them much more likely to act on those desires."

Caitlin thought about what he'd said and asked, "Uncle Richard, my husband James talked about men's biology and their weakness because of it. He believed that only a woman could help men to do the right thing!"

"Yes, it was true for me, but I realized it too late. Alcohol might be the hidden high that tears us all apart!" Richard told her.

"Thank you for all your wisdom, Uncle Richard! I really appreciate it. I hope you have a good night's rest in your new room. And if you're worried about disturbing anyone by going back down the stairs, Noelle's room is at the other far end of the hall, so you don't have to worry about making noise or disturbing anyone," Caitlin explained.

Richard thanked her and said good-night. Caitlin said she was going to bed and told him to sleep well.

A few weeks later, on the night before Noelle's first day at Somerton Elementary School, Caitlin lay in bed trying to stay focused on the joys to come the following day. She made sure that Noelle was well prepared and had everything she needed. She also started to think again about doing something different with her life, so she filled out an application in Noelle's school office for a job as a teacher's helper. She'd be able to work after she dropped Noelle off at school and remembered being a kindergarten teacher's aide when she was in the sixth grade. She'd loved it and still wished she'd been able to become a teacher. Next, she stopped by the William Nelson Law Firm uptown and filled out an application for a file clerk job with light typing skills. She'd found the job ad in the local newspaper.

Meanwhile, much to everyone's delight, Noelle thrived both in school and in the townhouse! Amelia once again said that her granddaughter was so smart that she might very well be a genius. Caitlin laughed heartily over her mother's unconditional love for Noelle and believed that her mother loved Noelle more than anyone else in the world.

Soon after she'd applied for the job, Caitlin was called for an interview at the law firm. After she dropped Noelle off at school that morning, she went straight to the interview. She and with five other women were given applications with test questions. Caitlin wasn't prepared to take a test, but she answered all the questions as best she could. Within a week she heard back from the law firm. She had the job! She'd start work promptly on Monday, working from eight to four. She was so proud that she'd passed the test and was sure it was all because she'd always loved to read.

The hours were perfect in the morning, giving Caitlin the extra time to drop Noelle off at school. But picking her up after school was going to be a problem. There would be an hour's gap between the time school got out and when Caitlin got off work. She'd have to find someone to pick up Noelle after school every day at three o'clock.

Luckily, Uncle Richard, upon hearing about this situation, offered to pick up Noelle. He saw it as a wonderful opportunity and it would be his most important responsibility. Everyone in the family agreed that it was the perfect solution. And they all believed this would be an exciting new beginning for Uncle Richard, too!

As it turned out, Caitlin enjoyed working for the law firm and felt that nothing was missing from her life. It was as if her dreams were being fulfilled from that day forward.

Meanwhile, Uncle Richard loved going to all of Noelle's recitals with Caitlin. He showered his little grand-niece with the tender love he would have given his own darling Emma. Caitlin believed that to Richard, Noelle was almost little Emma all over again. She also thought that he saw in her the same kind of love his late wife had shown to their own little girl.

Because he was so connected to Noelle, Caitlin asked Uncle Richard if he'd like to go to Noelle's school for the "meet the teachers" day because she couldn't get the time off from work. The purpose was for each class to gather and introduce family members to their classmates and teachers. Because Noelle loved Great Uncle Richard so much, Caitlin knew that her daughter would be happy to present him to her class. Uncle Richard had proudly said yes and immediately searched his closet for something nice to wear.

Caitlin made sure that he looked handsomely dressed by taking him shopping and helping him buy some new clothes. And while they were at it, she also took him to get his salt-and-pepper hair styled and brought up to date. Caitlin had always loved buying clothes and helping everyone dress well so doing this for Uncle Richard was as a labor of love.

On the appointed day, Richard met Noelle's classmates and her teacher, Miss Evelyn. Evelyn was very pretty, gracious, and middle-aged like Richard. She was especially fond of Noelle and told Richard enthusiastically about the little girl's liveliness and intelligence. Noelle seemed to be the apple of both their eyes. And when it was her turn, Noelle proudly presented Richard with a card that one of the sixth-graders had helped her make in class, and she read it to him standing in front of the whole class.

> Dear Great Uncle Richard,
>
> Thank you for picking me up at school every day and bringing me home. You are my greatest protector and you help everyone in our family to be happier. Thank you for coming to my school and

One of Seventeen

visiting my class, my teacher, and my classmates.

I know you're not my real dad, but I like to pretend that you are.

I love you!

Love,
Noelle

Evelyn's eyes were filled with tears as she listened to Noelle read her hand-made card to Richard. Richard's face was flushed with pride as he accepted Noelle's card and he said endearing words of gratitude to his beloved little great niece.

And when they sat down together for refreshments, Richard and Evelyn couldn't take their eyes off each other and spent the time getting to know each other a bit. Noelle happily went off to sit with her classmates, eating cookies and drinking juice while Richard told Evelyn about living with the Eden family and his job of picking up Noelle from school every day.

Evelyn told Richard that she'd never been married and had devoted most of her time to studying for most of her life. She had a PhD in Psychology but then decided to continue her education to become an elementary school teacher. She had no siblings and lived alone, and both her parents had already passed on. Their conversation was cut short when it was time for the children to go home, and they both were sorry to say goodbye.

Noelle couldn't wait to get home and tell everyone about Uncle Richard at her school. Richard was just as excited as Noelle to talk about everything that had happened at school. But he didn't say anything to anyone about falling for Miss Evelyn! He wanted to tell Caitlin about his feelings for the teacher once they were alone. He believed he could tell her and that she'd be the one person in the family who would understand.

Amelia called everyone to the table for dinner and asked Noelle to read the wonderful card she'd made for Uncle Richard she'd heard so much about.

After Noelle stood proudly in front of the family and read the card to everyone, almost as if she were saying grace, they all had tears in their eyes as they sat down to dinner. Caitlin never felt that Noelle was missing out by not having a father, especially as part of their large, loving family. But hearing Noelle's sweet words to Uncle Richard about considering him her father gave Caitlin's heart a bit of a tug.

12
No More Pretending

After dinner, Richard asked Caitlin if he could talk with her privately once she was done helping Noelle with her homework and of course Caitlin agreed.

When she was done, she went into her bedroom to unwind. She sat down in front of the typewriter and again tried to come up with the right words to write, but again, nothing came to her. But soon after, Richard knocked on the door and Caitlin invited him to come in.

Richard walked in and saw Caitlin sitting at her desk with her fingers on the typewriter keys, looking like she was in a trance. He didn't want to disturb her train of thought and said, "Am I interrupting, Caitlin? Because I can always come back."

"Oh no, Uncle Richard, I was waiting for you! Don't mind me. I'm still stuck with the same words and I can't get any further. So please, come over here and sit down."

Caitlin pulled another chair over for Uncle Richard and he began talking.

"Caitlin, I met Noelle's teacher, Miss Evelyn, today, and I have to say that I'm smitten for the first time since Isabella died! And from the look on her face, I think she felt the same way! "I still have some good years left in me, and she's not much younger, so I think that neither of us should wait too long to get together. So, I was wondering, do you think it would be alright if I invited her to have dinner with us soon? I haven't been with a woman for so many years. I'm afraid I might not know how to act or what to say if I took her out to dinner alone!"

"I think it would be wonderful to ask her to dinner with us, Uncle Richard!" Caitlin told him. "Maybe you can invite her to Noelle's birthday party next week, first. It's just the family and a couple of her new little townhouse friends."

"That sounds perfect, Caitlin!" Uncle Richard said. "Miss Evelyn's especially fond of Noelle because she's so bright, and I believe she has a soft spot in her heart, partly because Noelle never knew her father."

"Then I'll give you a birthday invitation that you can hand-deliver to Miss Evelyn tomorrow!" Caitlin told him.

"Great! Thanks so much," Richard said. "I really appreciate this!"

Then they said goodnight and he went to his room.

Richard quietly walked down the hall with Noelle's birthday invitation in his hand. He felt

One of Seventeen

like a high school boy, waiting excitedly for his first date with Miss Evelyn!

The following day, when Richard picked up Noelle from school, he made sure he hand-delivered the invitation. With a gleam in his eye as he handed her the invitation, Richard told Miss Evelyn, "Just your presence alone will be enough to make Noelle's birthday extra special. Besides, you're the hope for my future."

Miss Evelyn was delighted and quickly said, "I'd love to come to Noelle's party, Richard! Is there anything special I can get for her that you think she might like?"

"I'd love to help you out, but I really don't know, Evelyn. I'll have to ask Caitlin and get back to you," Richard told her.

That evening, Richard asked Caitlin what sort of gift Evelyn should get for Noelle.

Caitlin told him, "Now, that's even a good way for the two of you to get to know one another a bit more! Ask if you can take her shopping for her present. James and I got to know each other when I took him with me to buy school clothes for my younger brothers and sisters. He ended up taking me everywhere and it helped us find out that we were a perfect match!"

"And for a special gift for Noelle, I think anything Disney would be perfect. James used to talk about taking our children to Disneyworld one day!"

"Thank you," Richard said. "I think you're right. When I pick up Noelle from school tomorrow, I'll ask Evelyn to go shopping for the gift this weekend."

After that first shopping trip, Richard and Evelyn began to see each other often. For Noelle's gift, they decided on a Pinocchio musical doll that played "When You Wish Upon a Star." Evelyn also asked him to keep their relationship a secret for now because of the school's policy. She wasn't sure how to handle dating her student's great uncle. So Richard agreed not to tell anyone about his relationship with Miss Evelyn. Not even Carmen and Amelia would know about it at the birthday party. He knew he had to protect Evelyn until they knew the proper and legal way to handle the situation. But they both had no problem showing their love and dedication to Noelle, something they did without question.

But secret or not, Caitlin knew everything that went on between Evelyn and Richard because Richard kept her informed. He even confided that he'd asked Evelyn to marry him and that she'd happily said yes! But it had to remain a secret until they knew the right way to present it to the school principal. Caitlin told Richard that she adored Miss Evelyn from the first day she'd met her, too! And she couldn't think of a better wife for him.

After talking about his wonderful new love, Richard asked Caitlin about her own love life. He asked if she'd met anyone at the law office that she'd like to date, reminding her that it was already five years that she was a widow.

She told him that she'd met a very nice, intelligent, and handsome attorney who happened to be her boss. His name was William Nelson and he paid a lot of attention to her, going out of his way to be kind and to get closer to her every day. She said they often had lunch together and enjoyed each other's company very much. She said that whenever she went on her break, he was always right there, too, like he was waiting for her. She said he offered to pay for her lunch every time, but that she couldn't even think of getting involved with another man yet. "I guess I need more time," Caitlin said.

Richard was concerned and gently suggested, "Maybe you'd like to talk to Evelyn about this, Caitlin. She's been very helpful to me in understanding the traumatic experiences I've been through. And you've had so many losses, starting with your mother when you were just six, and then ending up in an orphanage and landing in and out of foster homes. And on top of it all the sudden, terrible loss of James! I believe Evelyn can help you, Caitlin. She has a PhD in Psychology and knows what she's doing."

Caitlin and Richard had tragic, parallel lives, and through their talks, she began to see that life could turn around after seeing him so happy and in love again. They were both so young when they lost their spouses. That had changed them, despite the different circumstances. Seeing Richard's blossoming relationship with Evelyn gave Caitlin hope. She even felt that those letters stored with her marriage license were somehow mysteriously working their magic!

And so, taking Richard's advice, Caitlin asked Evelyn for professional help to find a way to move on with her life, just as she had helped Richard to heal from his old heartbreak.

After the party, Amelia asked Caitlin when she was going to take her vacation since Uncle Richard surprised her and had generously given her and Noelle a a paid trip to Disneyworld

Caitlin said she planned to take her during the school's winter break. She'd ask her boss if that was okay and said he was always exceptionally kind to her and that he'd understand if she needed to take a couple of extra days off.

Amelia agreed and said that six was the perfect age for Noelle to go to Disneyworld. She was old enough to appreciate and remember what she saw.

Caitlin thought so, too, and said she'd framed the picture of herself at Noelle's age, with her brothers and sisters before Amelia and Carmen adopted them.

"I put in on her bureau to surprise her," said Caitlin. "I remember being six very well, and how

One of Seventeen

excited we were when you and Dad became our parents."

Caitlin knew that Uncle Richard and Miss Evelyn had secretly planned that generous trip for her and Noelle to go to Disneyworld, but she couldn't let her mother know she was part of that plan or that Evelyn was helping her to sort out her emotional hurdles and to understand herself. She couldn't talk about any of it yet. At least not until they knew it was in line with school policy.

～

A few nights later, Caitlin's father banged on her bedroom door. "Caitlin, wake up!" He said, sounding frantic. It was the middle of the night and he startled the whole family.

"Please come downstairs! Your Mother fell asleep on the sofa, and I can't wake her up," he shouted.

Caitlin hurried downstairs trembling and rushed to the sofa with her father beside her. She gently touched her mother's face and realized that she was gone.

In shock and disbelief, she mysteriously heard her mother's voice in her mind, saying that she was pleased with herself and the work she'd done here, but that she was very tired and ready for a long, peaceful rest.

And, miraculously from that day forward Caitlin accepted the sudden loss as a consolation, a peaceful departure, and a sign that Amelia's lifelong obligation and loving devotion were complete and that it was time to be with her own parents and beloved aunt after their long separation. Caitlin believed that Amelia had been a gift in her life and someone to model herself after, and that she was ready now at the age of twenty-six to move on and finally finish growing as a mature woman.

Meanwhile, Carmen was lost and overwhelmed without his beloved wife and all of his children gathered around to console him. It almost felt like Amelia was reminding them to help fill their father's void and comfort him now, when he needed them.

All of the Eden children and their families flew in from near and far for their mother's funeral. Each of them approached the casket and one by one they placed a rose on it as a symbol of their endearing love. There was a deep echo of loss and enduring love that long remained in their hearts.

With Amelia gone, Caitlin did her best to carry on with Amelia's nurturing spirit with Noelle, Carmen, and Richard. After working with Evelyn, she knew that she needed to move on from her sorrow. It needed to be over now. She felt that

One of Seventeen

James and Amelia continued to guide her and fill her with a new and growing hope.

❦

In time, everyone began to get past their grieving. Richard and Evelyn finally were able to let the world know about their relationship, and the school administration approved. With that behind them, they quickly announced their wedding date. They wanted a small wedding and asked Caitlin to be the matron of honor, with Noelle as the flower girl. Caitlin was so excited about the festivities that she took a chance and asked William, her boss, to be her date, something that Evelyn had warmly encouraged through her counseling.

Caitlin was at last ready to take a shot at romance once more and even wore the same dress that James had helped her pick out for their own wedding as well as for Julie and Anthony's.

When Caitlin asked William to be her date for her uncle's wedding, he told her he'd be happy to go anywhere, anytime with her. Caitlin was thrilled and knew right away by his sweet response that his feelings for her were genuine. When he looked into her eyes, she felt the same flutter in her heart as she'd felt with James.

Caitlin's relationship with William blossomed at the wedding, as though her dress still echoed a secret wish for romance. After the wedding,

Catherine Nagle

William and Caitlin became inseparable. They did everything together, and knew they were made for each other. Within a few months, William proposed to Caitlin and she said yes right away.

Some of her siblings worried that this marriage was happening too fast and much too soon after their mother's death. But Caitlin was sure and she didn't listen to anyone. She knew exactly what she was doing! She was free now and moving forward to start a new life with William and Noelle. She may have had other dreams for her future, but she knew that this life would serve her and her new little family very well. And she was sure that Amelia and James were smiling upon them.

All of Caitlin's sixteen brothers and sisters flew in again from near and far, but this time happily for her wedding. They gathered with their spouses and children, with their father, Carmen, her daughter, Noelle, and of course, Richard and Evelyn.

All of William's family and all of his and Caitlin's colleagues from work, and most of their lovely townhouse neighbors were there to celebrate with them. And Julie, the matron of honor, wrote a beautiful letter to Caitlin and William, which she read to them at the reception.

> Dearest Caitlin and William,
>
> You've brought your delight in love and wisdom to our family in

One of Seventeen

so many ways. You've counted all sixteen of your siblings as sixteen stars surrounding you, especially the biggest stars, our parents. You've enriched each one of us with your rare temperament of enhancing love all the time, showing that you were truly always a teacher at heart.

Caitlin, you showed us that bonding and belonging is the thing that we all have in common, wherever we come from in our lives. I have no doubt you and William will work together passionately, helping every orphan and widow that you meet at the law firm. Because, dear William, Caitlin won't let you rest until you do!

Caitlin, I'm so glad you moved forward with William! He looks as proud as a prince and you are as lovely as a princess, with sweet Noelle by your side.

Thank you for showing us that we must all remember to feel the love around us as well as from those who've gone before us. You've shown us how to trust again and to move ahead, toward everything good in life.

Catherine Nagle

Congratulations, Caitlin and William, and Noelle, too!

Caitlin, William and Noelle went to Disneyworld for their honeymoon. They even brought a nanny so they could have some time alone together. When they got back, they bought a new luxury townhouse named after the Eden family in honor of the estate that once had stood on that land.

A year later, William adopted Noelle. Caitlin continued working, but only part-time at William's law firm. She, at last, had plenty of time to take the courses she needed to get her teaching degree and certification. William's long hours at his law firm gave her time to study. And before long, she was successfully balancing her new teaching career and her family life, all with William's help. Their dear neighbor, Mary Kristopher, became Noelle's part-time nanny, an arrangement that Noelle thoroughly enjoyed.

The new little family remained close and frequent visitors to Caitlin's father, helping him with whatever he needed. They also spent time with the loving Marino family, who cherished Noelle, James's only child.

In her new home, Caitlin's corner desk still held the same stacks of papers piled high. They were her stories that at last sat next to her typewriter, which still held a blank piece of paper and the

One of Seventeen

worn-out ribbon used up by the many words that she had finally found.

But she'd had a lot of help. Aunt Evelyn, but though an angel, who not only had her doctorate in psychology, and was an expert teacher, also had been an English literature major. With that part of her training, she helped put together all of Caitlin's stories about growing up in a huge family. She planned to send them to a publisher on Caitlin's behalf and believed that the stories about life at the Eden estate would inspire hope in people who needed it. Aunt Evelyn knew that the stories were appropriate for the young and the old, but would be most helpful for anyone who'd experienced loss and wanted to create happier lives for themselves.

Evelyn helped Caitlin to see that she'd never been immature, despite what her family had believed. In reality, she'd simply been afraid. Her grief felt so much like fear. Evelyn explained that people like Caitlin, who had struggled so early in her life, grew more self-confident as they learned to be strong. She helped her to understand that her affections of doing for others gave her clarity to trust in the Golden Rule and to know that she's not alone. This helped Caitlin to be able to stand on her own two feet and get on with her life.

After two years of study and work, Caitlin got her dream job and finally started teaching at the Somerton School where she and her brothers and sisters had gone. She taught English and loved it.

But she would always be grateful to have been a waitress and to have worked alongside Julie and believed that those experiences helped her to become a better person. She felt that Amelia's nurturing and wisdom had helped to keep all seventeen children safe and happy all through their lives.

Carmen Eden lived in the same townhouse for ten more years until his peaceful natural death, believing that Amelia was calling him to be with her once again. Ellis handled all the funeral arrangements with love and dedication that was fit for a king. He was buried with full military honors befitting a soldier wounded in action, with taps played in a most moving service.

Carmen and Amelia had been through difficulties in their early lives, but they grew up and found each other and were very happy, especially after adopting all their children. Watching all seventeen children flourish helped them depart from life with a great sense of accomplishment and peace. Their huge family was grateful to their beloved parents for having created the most wonderful family for all of them.

Noelle remained a charmed only child until the day she married Shane, a most wonderful man, and moved out of her parents' townhouse at the age of twenty-five.

In time, Caitlin and William had a child together and named him Warren. And for the next

One of Seventeen

twenty-four years they started the cycle all over again, once again raising an only child. To this day, Caitlin still writes and is happiest when she's with her family.
  The End

DeNofa Family 1971: Parents and Seventeen Children

Carmen and Amelia DeNofa, Army 1940s

Photo Credit: United States Army

Oldest Siblings 1940s

500 Club, Oldest Sisters, and Sister-in-law 1950s

Photo Credit: 500 Club Atlantic City NJ Boardwalk
(Permanently closed, no forward address)

Sister, June DeNofa, Warren G Harding School 1960s
Photo Credit: Warren G Harding School

Catherine DeNofa, Frankford High School 1960s
Photo Credit: Barclay Studio

Sisters, and Sister-in-law 1990s

Natalie Matucci 1972
Photo Credit: Sears Portraits

William Nagle Jr. 1997
Photo Credit: J C Penny Portraits

Natalie and Sean Orlando, Wedding Portrait 1995
Photo Credit: William J Munizza

Christian and Angelina Orlando
Photo Credit: Joanna Snyder

Carmen and Amelia DeNofa 1971

Youngest Brothers, Louis, Ronald,
Thomas, and Charles 1960s

William Nagle Jr., Lehigh University Class of 2017
Photo Credit: Prestige Portraits

Carmen DeNofa Jr., Oldest Brother 1960
Photo Credit: Olan Mills Portrait Studio

(In Philadelphia, 900 Orthodox Street Permanently closed, no files are kept after two years)

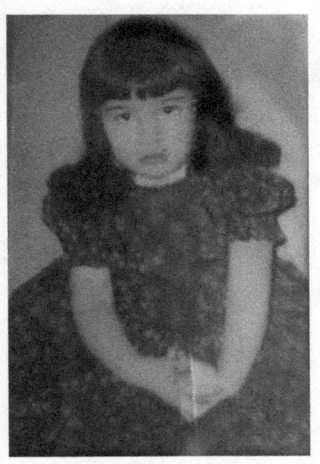

Shirley DeNofa, Youngest Sister 1961

Sister Faye DeNofa, Modeling Portrait 1960
Photo Credit: Olan Mills Portrait Studio

(In Philadelphia, 900 Orthodox Street. Permanently closed no files are kept after two years)

Carmen DeNofa, 74; a painter

By Donna St. George
Inquirer Staff Writer

Carmen DeNofa, 74, a Frankford mural painter who was "king" to his family of 17 children, 38 grandchildren and eight great-grandchildren, died Monday at Saint Mary Hospital in Langhorne.

Mr. DeNofa had married at 16, and started his large family in a rowhouse in the 1800 block of North Pear Street. Before moving to larger quarters, 17 children were sharing the house with two bedrooms and one bathroom.

The children had to stand in line, waiting for the bathroom, to brush their teeth. They had to eat meals in shifts. Money was tight.

"They were so young and so much in love, and they just had a baby every year," said Bea Garvey, 49, his daughter and the oldest of the children.

"... It was hard but it was a pleasant hard," Garvey said. "And believe it or not, they spoiled all of us. It was fun. It was a lot of fun. We were poor but when we did get, we got the best. They would do without for us."

A self-educated artist who never attended high school, Mr. DeNofa spent his workdays as a free-lance painter, finding jobs at bars, churches and the homes of the wealthy.

During more than 50 years of painting, he worked on projects ranging from the interior of St. Martin of Tours Church near Oxford Circle, the old Erie Social Club and The Little Spot bar in Frankford to private homes in Huntingdon Valley.

To earn a living, he also decorated and designed homes, and picked up other jobs.

"The guys he worked with, they would say that they learned more from him in one day than they learned from anyone else in five years," said his youngest son, Ronald, 21. "He would teach them, and have them do it the right way. He never did anything halfway."

Eventually, Mr. DeNofa's work afforded him a new home, this time in Northwood in the 1200 block of West Harrison Street — with six bedrooms and three bathrooms. By that time, in the mid 1960s, the children were moving out, and space was plentiful.

During one part of his career, his children said, Mr. DeNofa attracted the interest of Walt Disney Productions, which promised him numerous amenities if he would move to California to work.

Mr. DeNofa turned it down because his wife, the late Molly Quicci DeNofa, wanted to stay in Frankford, they said.

"That was the thing he enjoyed most — my mom and the kids," said his daughter, Bea. "He was special, kind and giving."

To his children, Mr. DeNofa was indeed a man of numerous attributes. Tall and sturdy, with black hair and a black mustache, he was strong, they said. Though he was never formally educated, he taught classes at the Philadelphia Art Museum from 1949 to 1953.

He was good at shuffleboard and darts, and had played the games in a number of bars, his children said. "But he would never touch a drop of liquor in his life," said his son, Ronald. "He was against it. Totally against it."

As Mr. DeNofa's children grew, he taught many of them his skills in business, construction and home decoration, they said.

"I'm 49, and I didn't make a move without saying, 'Daddy...,'" Garvey said. "He always knew the answers. He was our king. He really was a king."

In addition to the 17 children Mr. DeNofa reared, four others died while they were still young.

Surviving are daughters, Bea Garvey, Fay Konrad, Molly Ditro, Rose Webster, June Glenn, Cathy Nagle, Maryann Neff, Shirley Wircostoff, sons, Carmen Jr., Dominic, John, Ernest, Robert, Charles, Louis, Thomas and Ronald; 38 grandchildren and eight great-grandchildren.

A viewing is to be held from 7 to 9:30 p.m. today at Nulty's Funeral Home, 4292 Frankford Ave. A Mass of Christian Burial is at 10 a.m. tomorrow at Mater Dolorosa Church, Paul and Ruan Streets, Frankford. Interment is at Our Lady of Grace Cemetery, Langhorne.

Carmen DeNofa in the News
Philadelphia Inquirer 1988
Credit: Used with permission of Inquirer
Copyright 2019. All rights reserved.

CTOBER 11, 1958

18th Baby Crowds Home

At their cheerfully bustling rowhouse on Frankford's Pear st., Carmen DeNofa and his 16 children were preparing yesterday for what has become almost an annual event:

Mama is coming home in a few days, with a new baby. Mama is Mrs. Mollie DeNofa, 40, and she gave birth to her 18th child, a nine-pound, two-ounce girl, at Frankford Hospital Thursday afternoon. One of the couple's children died in infancy.

When she returns, Mollie will be bringing more than a new baby with her. She'll bring new problems. Among them, where to find room for the latest arrival, what to name it, and how to meet a milk bill that is mounting to astronomical proportions.

DeNofa, who is 42, earns his living as a commercial artist. His family long ago outgrew the six rooms in the house at 1839 Pear st., but he hasn't been able to save enough for the big down payment necessary for a house that would properly accommodate his family.

"Only the newer homes are available with a GI loan, and they are just too small," says the husband, who was wounded twice in action in Germany during the Second World War. "I need a six-room house—a six-bedroom house."

The porch of his present place, Carmen says, looks each morning like the loading platform at a dairy. He's getting 15 quarts of milk a day now, and with the new baby it'll be upped to 16 in no time. As for the family wash —well, he'd rather not think about it.

With the birth of a girl, the total number stands evenly divided—nine boys and nine girls.

"I'll spare you the old bromide about baseball teams in the family," said Carmen. "I'm as tired of it as anybody else."

What is the new little girl to be named? Well, Carmen and Mollie don't know yet. So far they've named Carmen, Jr., 22; Adeline, 20; Faye, 18; Molly, 17; Rose, 16; Don, 14; June 12; John, 11; Ernest, 10; Katherine, 8; Mary Ann, 7; Robert, 6; Louise, 5; Charles, 4; Thomas, 3, and Ronald, 2. What does that leave in the way of names?

Marilyn Better, Returns to Work

HOLLYWOOD, Oct. 10. (UPI). Actress Marilyn Monroe returned to work today on the set of her new picture, "Some Like It Hot," after a two-day absence caused by illness. She spent two days in bed with a "virus infection" and a temperature of 102 degrees.

Amelia "Molly" DeNofa in the News Philadelphia Inquirer 1958
Credit: Used with permission of Inquirer
Copyright 2019. All rights reserved.

William and Catherine Nagle, Florida 1990
Photo Credit: Royal Caribbean

About the Author

Catherine Nagle grew up in Philadelphia with sixteen brothers and sisters, reared by loving, old-school Italian parents. Her artist father's works graced churches and public buildings; her mother was a full-time homemaker. A professional hairdresser, Catherine worked in various salons while studying the Bible and pursuing spiritual growth through courses, seminars, lectures, works of C. S. Lewis and through various Christian conferences, including the National Theology of the Body Congress.

She is an ambassador of the Society of Emotional Intelligence, and a frequent contributor to the Huffington Post and Arianna Huffington's Thrive Global. The mother of two children and a grandmother, Catherine lives in Pennsylvania with her husband. She is the author of two nonfiction books, *Imprinted Wisdom* and *Absence and Presence"* and a novel, *Amelia*. Her work also appeared in Anne Born's *These Winter Months*.

About My Writing

I first started to write about ten years ago. I joined a wonderful online writing community, Red Room Writer's Society. On that forum, I learned a great deal from many remarkable, experienced, and talented writers. My first books were nonfiction and focused on family and spiritual beliefs and principles, and so do my blogs on Red Room, Huffington Post, and Thrive Global. Recently I began to try my hand with fiction, and it's been joyful for many reasons. I find it a more natural means to express myself.

I once read somewhere that Madeleine L'Engle wrote to inspire the young and also mature adults. She said in an interview that her genre distinctions are both real, *"They're different aspects of one reality."* I resonate my stories in the same way.

One of Seventeen, draws a clear picture of what it *really* was like to grow up in a family of seventeen children, a wonderful experience most people haven't lived through. Unlike in my own life, in the novel, I created a family of adopted children to do this.

I hope you enjoy reading *One of Seventeen*. Thank you so very much for reading!

Synopsis: One of Seventeen

Caitlin Eden is one of seventeen orphans adopted by a childless but wealthy young couple, Amelia and Carmen Eden. They adopted two families of children whose parents had either died or were otherwise out of the picture and created a warm and loving family for all of them. Caitlin was a naïve, timid young girl who was always anxious to please but also a bit immature for her age, even as she grew into a teen and young woman.

Eventually Caitlin fell in love with her brother's best friend, a charming commercial pilot who adores her. He marries her and makes her happy, but tragically dies in a plane crash, leaving her widowed and pregnant after only a brief weekend of marriage.

Meanwhile, her parents' financial setback forces her to set aside her plans for college and a teaching career. When her family decides to sell their estate to live somewhere more affordable, she discovers some long-hidden, heartbreaking letters from one of her father's long-lost relatives. This is part of her father's life that he's never told anyone, not even her mother, and before long the truth comes out.

One of Seventeen is an inspiring, heart-warming story that will appeal to fans of romance and anyone who has loved and lost and found love again.

Acknowledgments

Thank you to Evelyn M. Fazio, my remarkable editor, for your patience and teaching me that I can write, and not giving up on me, but believing in me. Love you!

Thank you to Balboa Press, and the entire team of professional consultants; Tiffany Taylor, Baylee Alexander, Marsha Manion, Mary Oxley, Ann Minoza, Theresa Irvin, Chuck Sison, Mariah Marcs, Dion Seller and Gab Richter for your support, patience, and kindest understanding. And for the entire design team of creating the most beautiful interior and the most intriguing book cover! Your artistic and professional talents have helped me to create and proudly publish, *One of Seventeen*. I am deeply grateful to all of you!

Thank you to Joanna Snyder, William J Munizza, United States Army, Royal Caribbean, Sears Portraits, J C Penny Portraits, Barclay Studio, Olan Mills Portrait Studio, Prestige Portraits, Warren G Harding School, 500 Club Atlantic City Boardwalk, for all your beautiful photographs and professional portraits that allowed me to proudly showcase your wonderful portraits of true works of art in *One of Seventeen!*

Thank you to the Philadelphia Inquirer, and staff writer, Donna St. George, and Aimee Gray, of the YGS Group, for the honor of allowing me to proudly showcase in *One of Seventeen*, both my parent's news in your famous newspapers!

Thank you to William "Bill" Nagle, my sweet husband, for supporting me with all my books and being proud of me! None of this would be possible without your depth of love that moves me forward. I love you!

Thank you to my beautiful children, Natalie and William Jr., and grandchildren, Christian and Angelina, for helping me to understand our modern world through your eyes that inspired me to write *One of Seventeen*! I love you more!

Thank you to my late beloved parents, Carmen and Amelia "Molly" DeNofa, for raising me with the same devotion as one would give an only child, along with my sixteen siblings in an extraordinary and most unbelievable family! I love and miss you very much!